WORK IN PROGRESS

Janice Tampa

CONTENTS

CHAPTER 1 (ELOWYN): I CAN TELL

I knew what I was signing up for. He'd never made any secret of it, but at the time, the tradeoff seemed...distant. Unlikely. Lachlan couldn't get enough of me, so I could never imagine he'd go somewhere else when he had me waiting at home, ready and willing to give him whatever he wanted.

But he'd warned me. In a vague way. "Sometimes I'll stay at the club. You don't ask me about those nights, or what goes on or what I've done or who I spent time with. But I'll always be careful and I'll always come home to you. It's just the way the biker life is. You have to be OK with it. You have to know that you're the one I love, you're the one I made my ol' lady and nothing else matters."

Considering the crappy family I came from, the poverty I'd lived in, the scrounging for food I'd done, the lack of stability I'd experienced, the dead-end jobs I'd worked since I was fourteen -- his offer sounded good. I'd seen the horrors my mom had put up with right in front of her, and his vague warnings didn't seem real. He'd bought us an adorable three-bedroom house and handed me his credit card and told me to make it our home. Then he'd given me a leather cut proclaiming me to be his property, he took me for rides on his bike and urged me to use the card for things I wanted. But I rarely did. I was happy with what we already had.

Then, right after our first anniversary, things had started to change. Lachlan started spending the occasional night at the club after parties I wasn't invited to. I'd get a text telling me he was staying at the clubhouse and he'd see me in the morning.

After the first couple of times he didn't come home, I began to panic, worrying he'd tire of me and set me aside. My pride hadn't yet kicked in. So I got a job two towns over in a place no one from the club would ever go to, during the hours he'd be at work. I told them I couldn't work weekends and never past five. But I was a solid, dependable worker, happy to come in at eight and get the store ready for opening. Soon, I was an assistant store manager and making some good money and I saved every penny. I'd opened a bank account at a credit union in this town that wasn't affiliated in any way with the bank where Lachlan and I had our accounts.

My man did work hard for the club, and he was gone from seven in the morning until at least six at night and he made more than enough for the two of us. I was frugal with his money, budget conscious with the meals I made and only rarely bought myself new clothes. Lachlan was still sweet with me, still caring, still took me out, but I was putting up walls in anticipation of him leaving me.

Two years went by, then three, then four, and now five years had passed. Every year, he'd slowly been spending more nights at the clubhouse so now he was gone once a month, sometimes twice. On those occasions I went to the club in the last year, I noticed one of the club girls giving me looks, then giving my man looks and I figured out they had something going. A couple of times, I'd noticed his eyes straying to her and I didn't like the looks between them. The arrangement I'd agreed to before I became his old lady was no longer working for me. I wanted to be someone's only.

As if the universe was sending me a message, I'd recently been offered a store manager position in another state and accepted the promotion. Lachlan was leaving for a club run and would be gone for a week, and the timing was perfect. I was afraid I'd have to take off while he was at work, which would make being discovered riskier. I bought a nice used car with some of the money I'd saved, and told them to have it detailed and delivered to my house the next morning, and for a small fee, they agreed.

The night before he left for his trip, he pulled me to him in bed and for the first time ever, I refused him.

"Is your girlfriend going on the trip with you?" I asked quietly.

"What the hell are you talking about?" he'd asked me, his voice impatient. "Only club brothers are going."

"I'm sure she'll be lonely with you gone for a week."

"What the fuck's gotten into you?" he demanded. I was heading into territory I wasn't allowed in and he didn't like it.

"I want more," I said simply. "What we have? The lies, the nights at the club with...well, it's not enough. I thought I could put up with it, but every night you spend away from me...it's killing me."

"You know I love you," he said, as if that was it. End of conversation. He didn't want to discuss it, so it was a forbidden subject.

"I don't like your version of love," I whispered and turned my back to him.

"You knew what to expect from the start. I was straight with you. Just remember, you're the one I love and live with," he said, then pressed a kiss to my shoulder. "Sweetheart, we'll talk when I get back, OK?"

"OK," I said. The one and only lie I ever told him. I wouldn't be here when he got back.

Early the next morning, Lachlan left and I followed him to the clubhouse, parking on the street, and watched. Sure enough, she came running out and kissed him goodbye like I'd refused to do. I'd turned my head and his lips hit my cheek, then he'd sighed in annoyance at me. But when I saw her jump into his arms, I knew leaving was the right thing. Sometimes you hurt so much, it doesn't even hurt anymore. It's just a part of you that you accept. Trading stability for my dignity and self-respect made me sick, especially since I'd let it go on so long.

After the brothers rode off, I drove home. My car was being delivered in two hours and I had clothes to pack. Once the three large suitcases I'd bought and hidden in my trunk were filled with my clothes, I put all of my shoes into two small storage bins and snapped the lids on. I carried them out to the garage, ready to load the minute my car was delivered.

Back inside the house, I tidied up, made the bed, and put the dishes in the sink in the dishwasher. I'd put my phone on the counter to leave behind with some other things, but then it buzzed with a text.

Already had to stop because one of the brothers didn't have a full tank. Didn't like the way we left things this morning between us. You know I love you and only you.

In reply, I sent Lachlan the picture I'd taken this morning of his girlfriend in his arms, their lips locked and her legs around his waist.

Yeah, I can tell.

Three hours later, I was on the road, leaving the state and my life for the last five years behind.

CHAPTER 2 (LACHLAN): NO HELP

The last hundred miles of the trip back home were taking forever. It'd been a shit week from the very beginning, even before the fucking trip had started. I'd had my first clue the night before when Elowyn had turned me down flat in our bed and brought up things she'd never once mentioned to me in the five years we'd been together.

I'd been wracking my brain to figure out what had flipped her switch, but couldn't pinpoint anything I'd done recently that would have triggered her reaction. Elowyn was my girl, always had been since the first time I'd seen her. First woman I'd ever wanted to make mine, first woman I took one look at and knew she was different and was going to be in my life in a permanent way. Only woman I had ever loved. When I'd explained the biker lifestyle to her, she hadn't backed away from me, hadn't even batted an eye. She accepted right off that sometimes I'd fuck other women, but I'd always come home to her.

And she'd never mentioned it in all the years we'd been together until the night before the trip.

Shifts and changes like that always raised my antennae and my radar was pinging.

Then, when I was leaving in the morning, she wouldn't let me kiss her lips, and she always returned my kisses, her soft mouth sweet and eager against mine. Always. Ping. Ping. Ping.

Instead, she'd told me to have a safe trip and waved good bye to me after I'd kissed her cheek, and I rocketed out of the driveway on my bike, my mood sour. Even the prospect of a day of riding didn't improve my mood, and I lived to ride.

We took off, and only an hour into the trip, one of the brothers signaled he needed gas, which irritated me even more. What moron doesn't fill his tank the night before a long road trip? While all of us topped off our tanks, I had time to shoot off a text to Elowyn, hoping to calm down whatever was bugging her.

Her return text surprised the hell out of me. She'd followed me to the clubhouse and took a picture of Yomi kissing me. The club girl had jumped in my arms and pressed her lips to mine before I could step back, before I could remind her that I didn't want her mouth on mine, that she wasn't allowed to initiate shit. Her hands were gripping my hair like it was the only thing preventing her from falling off a cliff and it took me a minute to break free. Long enough for Wyn to take a picture and read more into this than there was, had been or ever would be. I'd aimed a few pointed, poisonous words at Yomi before we left the MC compound and tamped down my irritation as we took off. Now, with everyone gassed up, our road captain was signaling it was time to move on, so I shot off a quick text to Elowyn.

Don't piss me off by reading anything into this bullshit that isn't there

Tucking my phone into my cut, I didn't have time to wait for her reply. When we stopped three hours later, I grabbed my phone so I could see what she'd said.

And what she'd said was...nothing. Elowyn hadn't answered but she had read my text. Once again, my radar was pinging because she always responded. We bantered, we argued, we joked; that was something we did. My girl had a sharp wit and I had a dry sense of humor and the two blended together well. What we didn't do was not reply to one another.

At every stop for the next eight hours, I'd text Elowyn and she'd read my texts...but she wouldn't respond.

You know I don't like games. Answer me.

You need to answer me

Why did you follow me to the clubhouse?

Answer me, Wyn. What's going on?

I hadn't been this angry since the one-year anniversary of Elowyn becoming my ol' lady. We'd gone out to a nice restaurant and I'd proposed with a simple, elegant diamond ring. It was pure Elowyn and the second I saw it, it reminded me of her.

Then she'd turned me down. Didn't even pause to think about it.

Being your ol' lady's good enough for me. I don't need or want a legal commitment.

She gave me the same answer every year when I asked her to marry me on the anniversary of her officially becoming my ol' lady. It always pissed me off when I brought up marriage and she shut me down, refusing to discuss why she wouldn't consider it other than saying she didn't want a legal commitment.

It was about two weeks after our first anniversary that I first stepped out on Elowyn. Spent the night at the club drinking with the brothers after a quick, successful run, feeling frustrated, like I wanted to shed my skin, without understanding exactly why and didn't say no when a club girl offered to wipe the scowl off my face in her room. After that, feeling more in control, I'd gone to my room alone, sent Elowyn a text saying I was staying at the club and stared at the ceiling all night, trying to drown out voices I didn't want to hear, fighting the urge to go home and get into bed with Wyn.

She'd been quiet when I'd come home early the next morning, where I found her in the kitchen with the coffee brewing and whipping up some eggs to scramble. I could smell the bacon in the oven and she'd already made biscuits, which were cooling. When Elowyn turned from the stove, there was a look in her eye that hadn't been there before last night. Not knowing what to say, exactly, we sized each other up for a few awkward moments before I finally spoke, realizing I needed to get us back to normal when I saw she'd only set one place at the table. Breakfast was always a shared meal. Every morning, without fail, she and I ate breakfast together, the same as we ate dinner together every night.

"Wyn," I began gently, pointing to the table, "I told you I'd always come home --"

"I know, Lachlan. I know," she said, and her crisp tone clearly let me know she didn't want any more words out of my mouth on the subject of last night. "I just didn't know when."

"Always in time to have breakfast together. Had a shower at the clubhouse but don't like the hard water there, so I'm gonna go grab a quick shower, change clothes. Then we'll eat, and we can make some plans for today, yeah? Maybe go for a ride? Stop by the garden center or whatever you want to do."

My girl loved gardening and was in the process of transforming our backyard into paradise, as she called it. My job was laying a brick patio and putting in an outdoor grill.

Taking a deep breath, she smiled at me, but it wasn't her usual big smile, and I knew I was the reason it was dialed back. "OK, Lach. Go shower off...the hard water and breakfast will be ready. There's enough for both of us."

And now, Wyn wasn't answering my texts, wasn't picking up my calls and I could barely concentrate on the MC's business.

My VP, Specter, took me aside during a break one morning. "Not sure what the fuck your problem is, Shadow, but get your head outta your ass and back in the game. If you fuck up the numbers, Prez'll kill you."

I did better, but underlying every business discussion, I wondered why Elowyn wasn't answering, why she wouldn't take my calls so I could explain that fucking picture. I'd probably sent her more than two hundred texts and made at least sixty calls. We'd never been out of touch this long. I had a prospect ride over to check on her, but he said her car was in the garage and there was note on the door for Uber Eats to just leave the food since she had popped over to a neighbor's.

Probably planning another event for our neighborhood -- cookouts, margarita nights, pool parties, book clubs, food trucks -- she planned it all with a few other neighbors who were as social as she was. When I had the prospect go back to check the next day, he said there was no food bag outside on the porch but there was a different note on the door telling her friend Marisol that she'd had to leave early for book club to grab some wine and she'd tried to text her to let her know, but her phone had been acting up and her texts weren't sending.

That should have reassured me, but my motherfucking radar was still pinging like crazy. The next day, we left bright and early for home, and I kept wanting Specter to go faster, get us home sooner. It was such a fucking relief to finally pull into our garage, right next to Elowyn's car, just after dusk, so I could lay eyes on her.

"Wyn?" I called out when I walked into the house through the back door. I needed to make this right with her. A week without talking with Wyn was seven days too long. "Elowyn?"

No answer and the house felt like it did when she wasn't home.

Empty and still. Completely wrong. As if the life had been drained out of it.

"Wyn --" I called again before my eyes focused on the kitchen island. Wyn's phone was there, plugged in, but that wasn't what made my heart stop.

It was her cut that was laid out next to her phone that drew my eyes.
I snatched up the note that was on top of her cut and read it several
times before it sunk in.

Lachlan --

I'm gone. I could see what was coming, and that's OK because I
realized I needed more. I needed to be the only one for you.

I wish you the best.

Elowyn

P.S. Maybe you can give this cut to your girlfriend. I was going to say
it's only fitting since she's already gotten a lot of what was mine, but
then I realized...you were never really mine.

Oh, fuck, no.

I flew through the house to our bedroom and threw open the closet.
All her clothes were gone. Her shoes were gone. I yanked drawers
out of the dressers and onto the floor when I saw they were empty.
Running to the bathroom, I saw her shampoos and body washes
were gone, and the drawers in the vanity were likewise emptied of
her makeup and hairbrushes. With a sweep of my arm, I pushed all
of my things on the countertop onto the floor.

At this point, I didn't even realize I was yelling her name at the top of
my lungs as if I could conjure her up, bring her back to me. Without

thinking, I ran out the back door to get on my bike, bringing up the tracking app for her phone...only to stop dead when I realized that, with her phone sitting on the counter, I had no way to track Wyn. No way to find her. Not the first clue where she was or how she'd gotten there.

I pulled up our banking app on my phone, but that was no help. The only transactions had been mine.

She was gone.

CHAPTER 3 (LACHLAN): A HUNDRED THOUSAND

For what felt like the millionth time in the last forty-eight hours, I ran my hands through my hair. At this fucking rate, I was going to be bald before the end of the day.

"How can you not fucking find her?" I demanded for what also seemed like the millionth time in the last two days. My brother was supposed to be a world-class hacker and tracker, and couldn't find Elowyn. She was out there who knows where and I had no idea if she was safe or even alive, and didn't that twist my gut. I always knew where she was. She was a homebody who didn't stray far from our neighborhood unless I was with her. Wyn loved our home and she especially loved the little community she helped foster.

When we'd decided to move in together, Elowyn had asked for a neighborhood with people our age in it and I'd researched neighborhoods and found this one, a small, quiet community of one hundred fifty homes. It'd had three homes for sale at the time, and of the three, Elowyn had chosen ours.

"It's not too big, Lach," she'd said. "And it feels just right to me, like it can be cozy and homey. And it has a great backyard that's a blank slate." She'd confessed to me that she'd always wanted a garden and had plans for turning it into a flowery paradise, complete with a fish pond.

The biggest selling feature to me was the three-car garage; I didn't need much more than that, so if the house made Elowyn happy, I was sold. Not wanting to risk losing the house, I'd put in an offer right away and we moved in before the month was out.

Those memories crowded my head, keeping me from focusing on Wyn's whereabouts. The second I'd realized I couldn't track her phone because she'd left it behind, I'd started knocking on doors, talking with her friends in our neighborhood, and met confused stares and shrugs and concerned expressions. As far as they knew, she was still at home. No one knew where she was or when she'd gone.

Until I knocked on Marisol's door after she got home, our neighbor to the immediate right and the one who was mentioned in one of Elowyn's notes that the prospect had seen on our front door. She was also Wyn's best friend in the neighborhood.

"Yes?" she asked, blank faced and slightly hostile as if she'd never seen me before, as if we hadn't attended dozens and dozens of neighborhood parties together over the years. But her very hostility told me she knew something about my girl.

"Do you know where Elowyn is?"

"Elowyn. E-lo-wyn," she tapped her finger against her lips, drawing out the syllables. "Sounds vaguely familiar. Can you describe her?"

"You do not want to fuck with me on this if you know something, Marisol. I just got home, she's taken off, and I need to know she's OK. Tell me what you know," I demanded.

"Oh, I know her new man's taking good care of her," she purred to me with a wink. "Really good care of her."

"What the fuck are you talking about?" I demanded.

Not possible. No way. There was just no way. Elowyn wouldn't -- would she? Marisol had to be lying. She had to be making shit up just to fuck with me.

"Should I repeat it slower so you can follow along?"

"Quit fucking with me, Marisol." If she'd known me better, my tone should have warned her I wasn't in the mood for her messing with me in the slightest.

"Great guy...well, as much as a cheater can be. Anyhoo, he's in an MC so that makes it all OK. Has an ol'lady, but they have an arrangement so he can step out whenever he wants and he wants with Elowyn. They're so damn hot for each other. When he pulls up in my driveway, she always runs over and jumps in his arms and plants a big kiss on his lips. So you can rest assured that on those nights you're away on club business, he keeps her busy, so to speak -- too busy to be missing her man and thinking about what he's doing at the clubhouse when she's getting a little somethin'-somethin'."

I felt my control slipping as my blood started boiling and was seconds away from putting my fist through the wall. Marisol had to be messing with me. Had to be.

Right?

"Where the fuck is she, Marisol?" I growled, trying not to get in her face.

She leaned toward me, her face an angry mask. "I don't know! She wouldn't tell me. Just told me she'd be in touch when she got to wherever she was going, and I'm wondering if it was Mexico or Canada because she kept mentioning her passport. And by the way, congratulations on fucking up the best thing to ever happen to you! She was so happy when I first met you two. But over the last few years, I've had to watch that happiness dim year by year, you thoughtless, cheating prick! She only told me everything six months ago and only because I pushed and pushed and pushed until it all came out. You stupid, stupid asshole!"

She stepped back and slammed the heavy door in my face. I stood on her porch, breathing heavily, fists clenched at my side, fighting not to lose control. In a few minutes, I turned and walked back home.

My phone rang, and I almost fumbled it as I grabbed it from my pocket, hoping it was Elowyn. My whole body slumped when I saw it was only Specter.

"Brother," he said. "Something going on you need to tell us about?"

In the two hours since I'd discovered Wyn had taken off, I hadn't told anyone in the MC yet that she'd pulled a runner, hoping I could find her or she'd return home before I called in the professionals to track her down. She had no money -- the two thousand I'd left her before I went on the club run was still sitting on the counter. She hadn't used her debit card or either of the credit cards, so I had no fucking clue what she was using for money. Unless she really was with a man and he was paying for everything. No way. No way. I felt sweat break out on my forehead as it seemed more and more likely that maybe she was with another man -- no. That wasn't Elowyn. She wouldn't --

She wouldn't do the same thing to you that you did to her?

"What have you heard?" I asked my VP sharply, just not ready to admit that my ol' lady had left me, not wanting to listen to that voice in my head. Fucking conscience.

"My wife got a letter from Elowyn. Was just delivered to the house. Few of the other ol' ladies got one, too. All four letters say the same thing. She appreciated their friendship over the years, wished she could tell them more, but wanted to let them know she was gone, she'd miss them and would be in touch once she was settled."

"Fuck," I bit out. "Where were they mailed from?"

"From town, Shadow. They were mailed right here in town."

"Shit." My voice cracked like I was going through puberty. I still had nothing to go on, and I was starting to lose my mind. Why had she suddenly changed our rules? Why was she now taking exception to our way of life that we'd had from the start? Had something happened? Like another man --

Raking my hand through my hair, I forced myself to calm my sweaty, voice-cracking self down.

But I kept circling back to Marisol's words. Could Elowyn really have a boyfriend like Marisol had said? No. I couldn't believe that. That wasn't...it would explain a lot...but I couldn't see it happening. No. Plowing my hand through my hair, I forced myself to calm down yet again. Specter had said something to me and I'd completely missed it as I thought about Elowyn having a boyfriend.

"I have no idea where she is," I confessed, feeling all sorts of idiotic at having to blurt out that Wyn had left me.

"That's not the only letter. One came to the clubhouse. Hand-delivered to a prospect. It was addressed to Yomi, and he brought it to me. Something seemed off, so I opened it and all the note said was you can have him."

Well, this just kept getting worse and worse. Fuck! My life had taken a one eighty in the last week and I felt like I was sinking in quicksand.

"Brother, we can find her. You OK with me getting Mother involved?" Motherboard was our club's tech expert, a world-class one who could find Elowyn in probably no more than five minutes.

Two freaking days later, Mother kept blowing my mind with bits and pieces he'd picked up about Elowyn but he hadn't quite found her. Yet.

"Would have helped, brother, that you told me she had a job," he'd scolded me like I was a fucking kid.

"She doesn't have job," I'd snapped at him.

"Dude, she's had a job for the last four years. How'd you not know that?"

"She doesn't," I insisted, wondering how I could have missed that my woman had a full-time job. For four years.

"She did. She has a bank account, too. Looks like only direct deposits for the last four years, no money taken out until this week when she bought the car I told you about."

His finger pointed at the screen, showing me the account number, the name on the account and the amount in the account.

"That's not our bank," I protested, but I couldn't deny that the account holder, one Elowyn Novak, had an account at a different bank.

"Holy shit," I said when I looked at how much she had in the bank. Over a hundred thousand in her savings account.

And that's when it dawned on me that not only had Elowyn left me, but she'd been planning to for years.

chapter 4 (ELOwyn): Burning Eyes

Other than a heavy stone sitting inside my chest where my heart had been, the last six weeks since I'd left Lachlan had been good. Well, fairly good. Definitely OK. Not horribly bad, really. You can either choose to let the hurt drive the car or sit it in the backseat. Attitude is everything and I was determined for mine to be good, positive, so I left that hurt bitch buckled in the backseat.

Each day I was getting stronger, learning to let go of the routines I needed that were so much a part of my life over the last five years. Most good. Just a couple that were...not. I was learning how to be on my own in a healthy way, in a way I hadn't managed at all before I'd met Lachlan. In a way I hadn't managed in one very critical way since I'd been with Lach.

It's funny the blinders you can put on to survive. I'd been drawn to Lachlan from the start. His massive body felt like a solid wall I could stand behind. Hide behind. His long hair, beard, tattoos leather and denim made him look dangerous. But despite the embarrassment I felt following the circumstances of our first meeting, Lachlan took care to put me at ease. He refused to let me ignore him, and he sat at the end of the bar every night I was working and watched me or talked with me, depending on how busy we were. It was a few weeks before I realized we were actually getting to know one another. I wasn't quite sure what to do with a man who didn't want me for sex. Considering the disappointing, pathetic men I'd allowed access to my body before him, I wouldn't have denied Lachlan.

But he'd denied us. For three months.

He was entirely different from the men I had been with before, as I jumped from one frantic, failed relationship attempt after another. I had no idea what to do with the respect Lachlan had shown me. Respect was a foreign word, a strange concept to me, something I'd thrown away in my desperate, mistaken attempts to find something even more important that had eluded me all my life.

Caring and concern. Love didn't seem attainable and I wasn't even sure what it was or what it looked like, but affection was doable and would have been entirely welcome and easier to identify. I couldn't imagine someone caring about how my day had been, if I got home safely, how I was feeling. But every night, when Lachlan walked into the bar where I worked as a barback, he'd watch me while I worked and chat with me whenever it was quiet. I suspected Lachlan was tipping the bartenders very well so they wouldn't mind if he was flirting a bit.

So suddenly, miraculously, after almost twenty-five years, caring seemed to be staring me in the face. He'd started following me home after every shift, unless he was out of town on his club's business. On those nights, he sent a prospect -- someone working to join the club -- to make sure I got home safely. I felt cocooned in his care and his pale blue eyes communicated something to me that I'd never seen aimed at me in my life. Lachlan wasn't beautiful in a traditional sense, but he was extremely attractive in a rough way. His smiles, though rare, were glorious. And the longer we talked, the more attractive he became to me, and the more I looked forward to winning a smile from the man.

I felt lighter when he was around, and the first night he kissed me, I relived that moment for years. Kissing had previously been brief, a means to an end, something guys did to get me into bed. But Lachlan's first kiss was like my first kiss ever. He'd brushed my hair back from face and pressed his lips to my temple and I heard him inhale. His lips moved to my cheek, the corner of my mouth and then he kissed me fully on the lips, his hands moving into my hair as he kissed me more deeply. When he pulled back, his teeth lightly nipped my lower lip and he looked right into my eyes.

"That was a perfect start to us, Elowyn," he'd said to me.

It was.

It had been.

A few months later, he'd told me he loved me, and I'd wanted to cry and gather up those three words and tuck them into my pocket for safekeeping. I loved that man but I never would have told him if he hadn't said that first. Pure and simple, I loved Lachlan right back. Because of him, I knew what love looked like from the way he treated me to the way he talked with me to the care he showed me. It was the most precious thing in my life, and I wanted to keep it close at all costs.

"Lo," I heard my name called, bringing me back to earth. Somehow, at my new store, everyone called me Lo. I didn't love it but I wasn't going to make a big deal about the nickname. It was better than some of the things I'd been called growing up.

Smiling, I turned to face the store manager who was training me to take over from her in just two more weeks. Since I'd arrived six weeks ago, I'd been her shadow, trying to absorb everything I could before she retired. Trying to focus on my new job instead of wondering if Lachlan even cared that I was gone.

Ugh. This was a big step for me, and I battled myself everyday to not call Lach and tell him about what I'd achieved. Keeping my job from him for the last four years had been a challenge but I didn't want him to know I was working and saving money so I could leave when he got tired of me one day. I honestly thought it would have happened before I finally left, given Yomi and her big mouth. When she'd cornered me in the hallway at the clubhouse one night and explained some basic truths I'd suspected, I knew my time with Lachlan was rapidly coming to an end.

"Sorry, Nia," I said, apologizing for getting distracted by thoughts of Lachlan. She and I went over some scheduling conflicts we needed to resolve before we sent it to the employees through the portal, and after half an hour, we worked them out. Then we went out to the floor to observe the cashiers and stockers.

"It looks like we're going to need to hire a couple more cashiers," she said. "We're really getting busy and --"

I never knew how she was going to finish that sentence because we were interrupted by the electronic chime of a customer entering the store.

And there, in all his badass glory, burning eyes trained on me, was Lachlan.

chapter 5 (Lachlan): I was on my way

"**G**ive me her motherfuckin' address!"

I had Mother by the neck, backed up against a wall. He'd found Elowyn, but he wouldn't give me her location so I could go to her.

"Stand down," a deep, deep voice said from behind me.

You never ignored what that voice was telling you to do. Ever. If the implied threat wasn't enough, seeing what he was capable of after someone chose not to listen was enough to make you do whatever you were told to do forever after. So, unwillingly, I released Mother, who immediately grabbed his throat, gasping for breath.

Turning, I faced my prez, trying to school my features. Butcher didn't tolerate any disrespectful attitudes or even looks and given his mood lately, I wasn't going to give him the fight he was looking for.

"Got a job for you," he told me. "I told Mother not to give you her address or phone number until you get back."

Fuck. This news was not what I wanted to hear and was the last thing I wanted to deal with right now, but I nodded, trying to keep the pissed out of my eyes.

"You, Orion, Specter and Trap are going on a road trip for a special assignment. It should take five or six weeks and I need you on top of the financials so I expect your head to be fully in the game. I'll hear if it's not. More importantly, you'll get dead if it's not."

This just kept getting better and better. Now I'd be gone up to a month and a half and had no way to get in touch with Elowyn, leaving her free to do all sorts of shit I couldn't think about. Maybe she'd think not hearing from me meant I didn't care that she'd left. Maybe that would push her to another man -- no. Mirasol had to have been yanking my chain. She had to have been.

I would hold onto that thought for the next six weeks whenever I had a quiet minute to take my head out of the game and think about Elowyn. But that wasn't too often because this special assignment required finesse, careful negotiating, subtle maneuvering...and our guards up at all times. Butcher hadn't been kidding; one wrong move and the four of us would be going back to our MC in body bags. Wasn't sure why Butcher wanted to get into bed with these guys, but I'd stopped questioning his methods a long time ago because you couldn't argue with his results.

But eventually, we were able to broker a deal that was even better than the outcome Butcher told us he wanted to achieve, and we were able to leave after six long, fucking weeks. It took us two twelve-hour days of riding to get back, and even then it was after midnight when we walked into the clubhouse. No matter what time you returned, you went right to Butcher to give him every single detail and he didn't finish with his questions for us until four in the morning. As we were getting up to leave, he saw my hesitation and knew what I wanted.

"You can ask Mother for her information tomorrow. I'll give you three days to handle your shit then your ass is back here." He gave me a stare. "Problem?"

I shook my head, uncertain if I could even get Elowyn to talk to me in three days. "No problem," I assured Butcher, wondering just how much of a lie that was going to be.

We walked out into the hallway, and I realized that all I wanted was to get home and catch a few hours of sleep in the bed I shared with Wyn, holding her pillow to me, and then get back here as early as possible to get Elowyn's address from Mother. Butcher turned toward his room without another word to me while I walked out through the common area, which, at this hour, should have been empty.

But Yomi was curled up on a couch, waiting for me, wearing next to nothing.

"Shadow," she called as if I didn't see her. Had no intention of talking to her, so I just kept walking toward the door.

"Shadow! I need to talk to you."

"What?" I asked. I couldn't believe her. She knew the rules. Club girls weren't allowed to approach a brother in the common room unless he signaled. Butcher enforced that rule like his life depended on it, and many club girls had been kicked out for not believing he meant it.

"You've been gone a while and I thought maybe you'd want to have some fun tonight," she said softly, pushing her hair out of her face.

"No." I turned to head toward the door again, but her hand caught my arm. Stepping back from Yomi, I knew she couldn't misinterpret the glare I was sending her.

"Did the rules change while I was gone?"

She looked taken aback by the venom in my voice. While I'd never been what anyone would call kind to her, I also never spoke to her with outright hatred.

She shook her head. "No, but...everyone knows El left you. Because you were with me."

"With you? Are you fucking delusional?"

"For the last year, you've only been with me when you need someone --"

"I am not with you by any stretch of the imagination."

"You only came to me, though. For a year."

"Because I picked your name out of a fucking hat! You could have been any of the girls for all I cared. It was just chance that I drew your name. You and I weren't a thing and if you fuckin' thought that, maybe you should have mentioned it to me so I could have set you straight. You knew I was with Elowyn. You knew she was my ol' lady and what that means."

Her face got a weird look on it and something clicked. "You never mentioned it to me...but did you mention your delusional fantasies to Wyn?"

With my accusation, she looked downright uncomfortable, and I felt my control slipping away and my anger burned through me like a forest fire.

"Tell me what you said to her."

Her eyes darted to the left. "I never...I didn't..."

"Tell me what you fucking said to her!" I bellowed, right in her face. She gulped and stepped back from me, but I'd had enough.

"Start talking," I lowered my voice, the threat level ramped up and she knew it. "And it better be the truth if you want to have any hope of staying with the club."

"I told her we were together," she said, shaking hard because Mayhem club girls learned fast the quickest way out of the club was by lying or talking to ol' ladies. "I told her you'd made me your girlfriend and you were exclusive with me because you fell in love with me."

"You not only approached an ol' lady, but you fucking lied to her? You talked shit to an ol' lady?"

Twisting her hands together, she nodded.

"And that shit you pulled the day we left for a run, you running out and kissing me, which you know I don't do -- why'd you do that?"

"I saw...I saw her car on the street."

Glaring at her, I pulled out my phone and called a prospect. "Get out here."

Two minutes later, a prospect walked into the common room, pulling his cut on over his T-shirt.

"Yeah, Shadow?"

"Watch this one pack her shit and then watch her leave the compound. Tell the guard she's permanently done and put the word out to the brothers that she's gone for good."

"Shadow!" she protested. "You said if I told the truth, I could stay."

"No," I said, and I knew my voice was lethal because that's how I was feeling, "I said if you wanted to have any hope of staying with the club, you'd better tell the truth. The shit I heard? You broke every rule we had and lied to my ol' lady. Nothing was going to save your ass after that."

I nodded to the prospect and he took her arm and walked away with her while she started crying.

Forget sleep. I stalked off to Mother's room to get Wyn's new address and other pertinent information.

Less than an hour later, I was on my way to Elowyn.

CHAPTER 6 (ELOWYN): THE BIGGEST ONE

Watching Lachlan walk straight toward me through the store was like watching a train come at me in slow motion. He might be a big man, but instead of lumbering, he moved like a track star. People moved out of his way, and I'm not sure he even noticed them he was so focused on me.

He came to a stop barely two feet in front of me. "Elowyn --"

I held up my hand. "I'm at work. Whatever this is will have to wait."

Frustration crossed those rough-hewn features, but he nodded sharply. "When're you off?"

"Guess you'll have to wait and see," I said without giving him an answer, then I deliberately turned my back on him and spoke to my boss about the new employees she thought we needed to hire. I watched her eyes follow Lachlan out of the store.

"Who was that?" she asked. "Anyone we need to worry about?"

"Not at all."

"OK, so we don't need to call the cops on him, but you still didn't answer who he was to you," she pushed. "Something tells me he's not your brother or cousin."

"He's an ex, Nia. But he's not dangerous or any kind of threat."

So, I was lying through my teeth. Lach could definitely be dangerous. The first time I'd met him, there'd been something in his eyes that told me he was more than capable of hurting or even killing someone. And then I'd seen him in semi-action before I even knew his name.

I'd been out back on my break, on my knees, giving one of the regulars who came to the bar a blow job. Except tonight, Tim had decided he wanted it a little rougher than I appreciated, making me gag once too often, and he was ignoring me trying to push him back to get him to ease up just a bit. I was about to handle it with my patented twist to the balls -- this wasn't my first rodeo by a long shot, and I knew how to make them stop -- when Tim was yanked away from me and shoved up against the bricks.

A dangerous looking man in worn jeans, a black Henley and a leather cut pressed his forearm against Tim's throat. "Since you like blocking airways, let me return the favor," the stranger said. Tim couldn't answer, and the man pressed his forearm repeatedly against Tim's throat in pretty much the same rhythm Tim had been using on me. In no time, Tim had involuntary tears streaming down his face and was desperately trying to dislodge the man's forearm arm from his throat, but nothing short of a bulldozer was going to move that muscled arm.

Without stopping what he was doing, the man looked over at me. "You OK?"

I nodded, looking down, completely and thoroughly embarrassed that this man had seen me in such an intimate situation, and in the back alley of a bar no less, which just screamed class. I was wondering what he now thought of me, and equally curious as to how long he was going to keep fucking with Tim.

"What's your name?" he asked me, his voice low and a bit gravelly.

"Elowyn," I said softly.

"Never heard that for a name. I'm Shadow."

"Never heard that for a name," I tossed back at him, realizing he wasn't acting like he thought I was some slut. In fact, the way he was acting toward me was making my humiliation fade fast.

He grinned at me. "Go inside. You don't need to be here for the rest of this."

At that, he stepped back from Tim, who fell to his knees, hand at his throat.

"You're not going to, um, kill him, are you? It was consensual."

"Looked to me like you were trying to get him to back off."

"He was being rougher than usual, but I had it under control. I was about to use my patented move on him." And I made a yanking, twisting gesture with my hand that let him know what I had been planning.

The earned me another grin. "I'm not going to do anything permanent to him," he promised. "I'm just going to have a chat about manners."

"A chat. About manners?" I knew I was right to be skeptical.

"Yeah, I'm a real stickler for eti-fucking-quette. Now go inside."

I went inside and stopped off at the ladies' room to rinse my mouth, wash my hands and fix my hair before I clocked back in. A few minutes later, Lachlan came in and sat at the end of the bar, his eyes on me.

"Beer. Don't care what kind," he told the bartender.

"How'd it go, Miss Manners?" I asked, placing a napkin in front of him.

The bartender set Shadow's beer in front of him and walked away.

"Miss Manners," Shadow laughed once, shaking his head. That was the first night he sat at the bar and watched me while I worked but it wouldn't be the last.

"Lo?" my boss called my name.

I shook my head, and detoured off Memory Lane and back to the present.

"Sorry, Nia. I was just surprised to see him."

"He's a yummy ex, but I guess you already know that. I'm thinking it doesn't look like he got the ex memo, though. You sure he's OK? He won't try anything with you, hurt you or...?"

"Lachlan would never hurt me," I assured her, laughing to myself at the irony of the lie I'd just told her. Lachlan had delivered the worst kind of hurt I'd ever experienced in my life: he'd broken my heart, something I'd never let someone do in a romantic way before.

Four hours later, done working for the day, I walked out to my car and wasn't surprised to see Lachlan next to it, his bike parked in the spot next to my car. As he had in the store, he walked right up to me.

"I don't even know where to start or what to say to you, Wyn, and that's never been a problem with us."

"I don't know how true that is," I said, and he knew exactly what I was referring to.

"Let's go somewhere and talk."

I gestured to the parking lot. "Here is fine. There's not a lot to say."

"Elowyn," he said, and his voice was rougher than usual with frustration. "This is going to be more than a two-minute conversation in a parking lot. We have a lot to talk about."

What to do, what to do?

"Is it because I left and you didn't get to end it? Is that why you're here?"

That actually made him step back. "What the fuck, Wyn? Is that what you really think? You left without warning, without talking to me and you think I'm not going to try to fix things when the woman I love just walks out of my life?"

"Oh, no! Yomi left you?"

That got me a very irritated look because apparently someone wasn't in the mood to appreciate my humor. "Yomi lied to you, Elowyn. What she told you was bullshit."

"How do you know what she told me?"

"She told me and it wasn't hard to put together, especially after that fucking picture you sent me. She saw your car on the street, by the way, and decided to give you a show that morning. That's all that shit was. You're the only woman I've ever kissed, Wyn."

"Her lips on yours kind of makes that a big, huge lie."

"She kissed me, Wyn. I pushed her off as soon as I could get her motherfucking claws out of my hair and let her know what a mistake she'd just made."

"Well, obviously she felt comfortable enough to approach you since you'd been exclusive with her for a year and made her your girlfriend."

"That is exactly why we need to talk and it's going to take a while to work through things, so let's go some place to eat or go to your place, I don't really give a fuck where, as long as it's some place we can talk."

I thought about it for a minute, and realized that I actually had a lot to get off my chest, so maybe a talk would be a good way to end things once and for all and then both of us could move on. Somehow.

Since he'd found me, I knew that he already had my apartment address, knew what kind of car I was driving, where I worked and what my new cell number was.

"Fine. Let's go to my place and talk."

"I'll stop and pick up some pizzas, OK?"

Since I was hungry, I agreed. We could be civil about this last conversation between us and it would put Lachlan in a better, more accepting mood, I hoped, since he had this thing about feeding me.

"All right. See you when you get there."

When I went to get in my car, he called my name.

"Yeah?"

"I missed you, Wyn."

I stared back at those eyes that seemed so sincere and intent and strengthened my resolve. "You'll get used to it."

He frowned, definitely not liking my answer, but it was nothing more than the truth. He'd have no choice but to get used to my absence.

I drove away, Lach right behind me until he turned for the pizzeria that I liked -- I wasn't surprised by that in the least. I'm sure he knew where I bought groceries, got my gas, and had my hair cut, too. He obviously knew where I got my coffee since I worked there.

Making my way up to my apartment, I took off my work clothes and changed into my favorite jean shorts and a soft T-shirt. I tidied up the one bathroom, and made sure everything else was neat. Habit, I supposed, because Lach had always come home from work and told me how nice it was to come home to calm and not chaos.

Then he'd kiss my lips softly and pull me into his arms for a hug, and I would forever associate the slight scent of motor oil with comfort.

"No," I said out loud in the silence, not entirely sure what I was objecting to or why I was even putting that out there in the universe.

Thirty minutes later, Lach knocked on my door. When I opened it, he stood there, eyeing me with relief -- had he been afraid I wouldn't be here? -- and he walked past me when I stood aside. He took in my apartment and nodded once.

"Looks nice, Elowyn. Homey."

I took the pizzas to the kitchen counter and opened the boxes. One was my cheese-only deep dish pizza and the other was a garbage pizza. Lachlan liked everything on his pies.

"Let's just eat and then talk after," he suggested, and I was fine with that. No need to ruin my enjoyment of good pizza with depressing shit.

I ate two pieces before I was stuffed, but Lachlan worked his way through his entire pizza and a slice of mine. Once he was finished, he looked at me, and I knew it was about to get serious.

"Let's start with Yomi and her lies," he said, jumping right into what was a huge issue between us.

But not the biggest one.

CHAPTER 7 (LACHLAN): FIVE YEARS OVERDUE

"OK," Elowyn said. "Tell me all about your girlfriend and her lies."

"Can we go sit on the couch?" I asked.

She shook her head and indicated the small four-person table we were seated at in her tiny dining room area.

"I'm fine here. We don't need to be comfortable for an uncomfortable conversation."

"She's not my girlfriend. Not even close."

"Well, that's not what she told me. She said you'd been exclusive with her. For a year. How is that not girlfriend material?"

"Yomi's a liar, Wyn. Plain and simple."

"She told me you'd made her your girlfriend and you were exclusive with her because you'd fallen in love with her."

"Well, that's the biggest crock of shit I've ever heard in my life."

"So you weren't exclusive with her?"

"I was but not in the way you're thinking. About a year ago, one of the brothers was away on club business. He brought back an STD and one of the club girls got it and everyone freaked the fuck out."

"Oh, my God," she said. "I'm so glad I always made you wear a condom."

"No, Wyn, I hadn't -- hadn't been with anyone since he brought it back. We all got tested immediately whether we had a need to or not, and I was clear. But Butcher got pissed, called church and threw down a hat with all the club girls' names in it. He told us to pick a name out of the hat if we were going to mess around with them and whoever we picked was the only girl we could be with and no other brothers could go there with her. Whatever names were left in the hat, those girls had to leave the club. Butcher said if anyone fucked with his rule, he'd be getting rid of all of the club girls."

"And you picked Yomi's name."

Her voice was so quiet I could barely hear it, but I heard enough in it.

"I did."

"So you fell in love with her?"

"You'd have to talk to someone to fall in love with them, and I was already in love with you."

"In a year, a whole year, you're trying to tell me you didn't talk to her once?"

I hated talking about this. I hated that look in Elowyn's eyes. I hated that I'd driven her away. I hated every single thing about this because it was my own damn fault.

"I'll tell you what it was like, Wyn. I don't want to, but I will so you can understand that she was lying and so you can see exactly what it was and what it definitely wasn't."

I signaled to Yomi and stalked to her room. Unzipping myself, I rolled on a condom.

Knowing the drill, she pushed her shorts down, kept her back to me and and put her hands on the wall. She knew to keep them there.

"Shadow --"

"Shut it."

I pushed into her, my hand on her neck to keep her from trying to turn around or touch me. After a few strokes, I pulled out and finished myself off with my hand. Taking off the condom, I tied it at the end, zipped myself up and left her room, going directly to mine. Throwing out the condom, I washed my hands, disgusted with myself, then I tore off my clothes and showered in the hottest water I could stand, staying under the spray until it turned cold. After drying off, I walked to my bed and sat on the edge, head in my hands, trying to shut out the voices from my past.

"Every time was exactly the same, Elowyn. She was trying to fuck with you, to make it seem like it was more than it was. How she got a relationship out of that shit and my rules, I don't know."

"Rules?"

If I felt sick talking about this, I could only imagine how Elowyn felt having to listen to what an asshole her man had been.

"Yeah, my rules: no talking, no kissing, no touching, no oral, no foreplay, no being on a bed or anywhere except against a wall, no face-to-face fucking, no unprotected sex, no making her come, no coming inside her and as soon as I made myself come, I left."

Even though the rules were linked to my need for control, hearing it put like that made me face just how fucked up I was, how fucked up what I'd done to Wyn was. For a minute, I thought I was going to get sick and my eyes shot to Wyn's to make sure she was OK.

"You warned me," she said dully. "And I signed up for it."

I had, and she had, but that was absolutely no comfort now. None. Even before the warning I'd given her, I'd hinted at it, held us back from a formal commitment. Or maybe we'd both held back for a while."

I've never been with anyone like you," Wyn had said one night when she was cuddled up against me on my bed. I was sifting my fingers through her hair, just enjoying having this woman so close to me. I had plenty of experience with sex, but I'd never had the calm after the storm like this. As soon as I was done, I was gone. With Elowyn, it was different. She settled me, calmed those words that rattled around in my head and helped dr0wn them out with her surprising tenderness.

"Just a sec," she said before jumping out of bed, and I enjoyed watching the curves of her body move gracefully as she grabbed something out of her purse and hopped back up on the bed right next to me.

She put a small, wrapped box on my chest. "You probably don't realize this, but we've known each other for a year. Today, I mean. It's been a year today. Since we met."

Wyn was adorable when she got flustered and stumbled nervously over her words.

I looked at her and picked up the gift. "What is this?"

She smiled, and I realized how light she made me feel. "Open it."

I sat up and just indulged in the unfamiliar feeling of being given a gift for a minute, but then, looking at her eyes shining with excitement, I ripped off the wrapping paper and opened the box, where there was a braided leather wrist band.

For a minute, I couldn't say anything.

"Don't you...do you like it?"

I looked into her face and knew I wanted to look into those eyes for the rest of my life.

"I love it," I said simply because I knew if I tried to say more, I'd fucking lose it. I wrapped it around my wrist and had her join the ends of the clasp. I put my hand at the back of her head and pulled her down to me for a sweet kiss. Then, twisting, I opened my nightstand drawer and pulled out a little gift wrapped box. It was the first gift I'd ever wrapped so it was nowhere neat as hers had been.

"I know exactly how long we've known each other, Wyn. It's been the best year of my life."

She opened her gift and lifted the lid on a pair of little aquamarine studs.

"It's your birthstone, and you said once that this color reminded you of my eyes." And damn if I didn't start blushing like a nun who'd just heard a dirty word for the first time.

"I love my earrings," she said, giving me a deep kiss. "Thank you, Lach."

"I want to give you more, Wyn. I just don't know if I can be faithf--"

"No. Not today." Her voice was firm. "Today, we're celebrating. We have time for that talk later if we decide to get serious. For now, we are what we are and I don't want anything more. It's too much pressure for me to deal with."

"I thought we were going to talk when I got back, straighten out the Yomi situation and our other issues."

"It was time to go," she said simply, and I panicked inside hearing that.

"For four years you had this other job. How did that happen? I feel like I should have known this but you were never not home when I was. I was blindsided when Mother told me you'd been working for four years."

She shook her head. "I made sure you didn't know. I left after you did in the mornings and I got home before you did at night. I told them I couldn't work weekends. I left my phone at home but forwarded my calls to my second phone that I got to use when I left the house.

I got my own bank account in a different city and put every penny I earned in that account. When you asked how my day was, I just said it was fine and I told you about the things I did between the time I got home and you did."

"You were planning to leave me for four years, Wyn."

"It wasn't planning to leave so much as getting ready to go when you got rid of me. I knew that was coming after you proposed to me and I turned you down. I knew that was definitely coming when Yomi told me you'd made her your girlfriend. And even if she hadn't told me that, you would have eventually gotten rid of me. It was just a matter of time."

"I never would have ended things with you, Elowyn. Never."

"Well, it didn't seem like that to me. And what if I'd pushed about the other women, Lach? Every time I brought it up, I admit I didn't push the subject and let it drop too easily, but you clearly wouldn't talk about it. Just your usual spiel about how you'd always come home to me. You're seriously telling me that if I'd put my foot down, you wouldn't have ended things?"

"No, I wouldn't have ended things. Not with you, Elowyn. But I would have liked the opportunity to figure out a way through it."

"You could have talked to me. You knew I wasn't happy with the arrangement."

"I felt like you've always had a foot out the door."

"Because you wouldn't be faithful to me."

"No, Wyn, it was even before we had that talk. Almost from the start."

"Why couldn't you be faithful, Lachlan?"

That question was at the heart of everything and the answer to it was about five years overdue.

CHAPTER 8 (ELOWYN): HANDLE IT

* ****TW for child abuse reference*****

Lachlan looked at me when I asked him why he couldn't be faithful as if I'd asked him to explain the meaning of life or solve some incredibly difficult math problem. He shot to his feet and filled my little dining room space with his sheer bulk.

"Wyn, I want to just say because I'm a stupid dick and let it go at that. You don't know how bad I want that. Just forget the past shit and figure out being together again."

He looked at me with serious eyes, and I looked right back at him, not willing to give him a pass. Of course, that meant I wouldn't get a pass, either, if he pushed, if we began sharing our histories.

"But I know I owe you more than that. We've been together for six years, officially together five, and we've never fuckin' talked about our pasts. I've been good with that since I'm not really the type to talk about shit and you aren't really either."

That was the actual truth. Why revisit the past? Unless it was to stop letting it control your present and future.

"Lach, we don't need to talk about it since we're done --"

"No!" Lach's normally deep voice was almost shrill, as if he was panicking. "I can't stand here and listen to you say that. I don't want to be done. Wyn, you know I love you --"

"No, I don't, Lachlan. I don't believe that you love me, and maybe you never did. We worked for a while, but you're not enough for me anymore. What you're offering isn't enough anymore. I want all of someone, not someone who shares himself. When we first got together, I thought I could handle you cheating on me, but from that first time you spent the night at the clubhouse, it hurt. It hurt me knowing you were with other women and I wasn't enough for you."

He came right over to my chair and hunkered down next to me, clutching my hand in his.

"No, Elowyn. No. You were always enough for me. You have it backward -- I wasn't enough for you, and I knew you'd leave me one day.

But you were always enough for me. You're everything I ever wanted in a woman."

"Lach, I spent every day of the last four years just waiting for you to tell me to go. That's why I got the job and hid it from you. I was afraid if you knew I was working, you'd tell me to go sooner. So I saved all my money to give me a fresh start, a cushion, for when you didn't want me any more. And it was coming. You know it was. Every year you spent more nights at the clubhouse than the year before."

"Because I felt like I was losing you, Wyn. I felt it." I'd never heard Lachlan sound like this. He was always sure and confident and his voice was never shaky. "I knew it deep down, and the nights at the clubhouse made me feel in control for a bit. I had no control over you, I couldn't force you to stay with me if you really didn't want to, but I needed to feel some control."

"You were practically pushing me out the door, Lach! The other women, Yomi. I saw the way you looked at her when we were at the clubhouse for parties. All the hot looks whenever she came into the room, the way your eyes tracked her every move. I'm not blind."

"What the fuck are you talking about? I didn't look at her like that! That bitch meant less than nothing to me. I wasn't attracted to her at all."

"For a year you were with just her and you never felt attracted to her? So how'd you manage to have sex with her then if you weren't attracted to her?"

"Already told you how it was with her and the others before her. I gave 'em my rules and they did what I asked. It was just about having control, not about being with them. That's what I got off on. If I was giving looks to Yomi, it was because I didn't want that bitch coming anywhere near you, and I was warning her off, to keep away from you. And I tracked her movements to make sure she wasn't working her way over to you and maintained her distance. But I can guarantee I never once looked at her with heat."

I shrugged, not knowing what to believe, but finding it hard to wrap my head around sex for control.

Then it hit me.

I'd done the same thing with sex not for control but for affection. For approval. For praise. It never lasted past the guy zipping up, but I'd craved every so good, baby or you're a great fuck or never been sucked that good. Before I'd met Lachlan, the men I was with were my attempt to find someone to care. Even after Lach started sitting at the end of the bar, I'd still go out back on my breaks. And I'd look up and see Lach hidden in the shadows of the doorway.

He never called me names for doing what I did, never once judged me, but he waited and listened when I went out back to make sure none of the guys got out of hand. They didn't, maybe realizing Lachlan was hovering nearby like a guardian angel, but if they had, he'd have been right there for me. When I was done, Lach would walk me down the hall to the bathroom and wait for me, then take his seat at the end of the bar while I finished my shift. After a month or so, I simply stopped going out back on my breaks. I'm sure Lach noticed, but he never said a word, just continued to watch me while I worked and then he'd take me home at the end of my shift. Lachlan was showing me something back then, but I wasn't sure what.

"Why didn't you ever stop me, Lach? Tell me to not go out back with those men?"

He'd looked at me, holding me close on his lap and pushed my hair off my neck so he could press a soft kiss below my ear. "Got no say over you, Wyn, then or now. You had to stop on your own. I didn't mind waiting for you."

"But you stood by and listened --" I'd cringed at the thought.

"Couldn't make sure you were OK if I wasn't nearby. That was more important to me than anything."

"It just...what I was doing wasn't right. I mean it wasn't for the right reasons. It was for stupid reasons."

He'd tucked my head against his chest. "We all have our own ways of slaying the dragon."

Held in his arms, sitting on his lap, his heartbeat under my ear...I'd felt like I'd found someone to care, but didn't quite yet realize that his way of slaying the dragon would end up slaying me.

"So you have an issue with control." No question, just a statement to him. Lach got up and started pacing around the dining room table.

"Fucking hate this. I'm not going to get into all the details, but here's the basics. Took one intro to psych class in college to meet my gen ed requirements for my finance degree. The professor usually put me to sleep, but one day he was lecturing us about common issues people struggle with and swear to fuck he was looking right at me when he started talking about control issues. He said people who are scared of being at the mercy of others can gradually develop a need to be in control. Could be control over one particular thing or a bunch of 'em. And then he said it can come from some traumatic shit. Like if you're a kid and some big thing hurts you or scares you, stuff like that. Well, that was my entire fucking childhood. My mom died suddenly, then my dad's mom did right after, then my mom's mom, and so, given all that loss, my dad wasn't making the best decisions. He started moving us around, like ten times from the time I was eight until I was eighteen, making me leave my friends, my schools -- and he was always chasing after new girlfriends to try to take mom's place.

I had no say in my life. None. When my dad proposed to mom's first potential replacement, she left him. He proposed again to someone else less than six months later, and no surprise, she left, too."

In all our years together, Lachlan had never mentioned one word of it to me. This was all brand-new information. Then I thought of all the brand-new information I could offer to him and it was no wonder we never wanted to share our shitty pasts.

"Dad proposed again. She took off, too. He blamed me in all sorts of ways that hurt. Smacked me around while he told me women didn't want to stay around a kid that wasn't theirs. Then he said if he could get 'em to marry him, they'd stay. Told me every time he proposed that if a woman was willing to marry you, she'd be willing to stay with you. Heard that for fucking years through his additional marriage proposals, and they all eventually left before they married him."

"How many?" I asked, and he shrugged.

"Lost count, but every time dad said we were pulling up stakes, I knew another woman had dumped his ass and he was leaving to start fresh and find a new one. It was his way of being in control, I realized. So when I grew up, I looked for ways to stay in control. Some small way and it became sex. Sometimes I'd do somewhat normal sex, but most of the time, I had all these rules in place to control the woman.

Not until you, Elowyn did sex become something intimate. You were the only woman I didn't want to control like that."

"But you tried in other ways," I said. "Refusing to discuss your cheating was a way to control me."

"I never thought about it like that but I guess it was. I'm sorry about that, Elowyn. I don't like talking about all that shit, and I'm not offering it as an excuse, but I wanted you to know."

"So because I wasn't willing to marry you after you asked on our first anniversary together...in your mind, I wasn't going to stay."

"Yeah. And it ate at me for a couple weeks, thinking you were going to leave, and that feeling of needing control started itching at me for the first time in a long time. You were going to leave me and I didn't know how to handle that."

"And now I have left you, Lachlan. And I'm sorry, but you're going to have to figure out how to handle it.

Chapter 9 (Lachlan): A Plan to Win

Control is an illusion, and like any great magician, I performed one motherfucking trick after another. Too many to count, really. All my life, I'd craved control, waiting for the day when I was no longer helpless and without choices, able to exert control over my life. I wasn't one that had to have it in every aspect of my life but found that sex did it for me. I could control the woman I was with. I'd lay out what I expected beforehand to her, what I wanted, and if she agreed to the terms, there it was. I had control. Sex was less about pleasure and more about control for me. The few times I'd stepped outside my rules, sex had been mediocre at best. The limited pleasure I'd found hadn't been worth giving up my rules for.

Until Elowyn. Only for Elowyn had I ever been willing to give up my sex rules. Only with Elowyn did sex become a way to express what she meant to me, and it had nothing to do with control. It was about wanting her near me. It was about craving closeness, not control. It was about fucking feelings and what the hell are you supposed to do you do with those? Emotions were an entirely different world to navigate.

Night after night after, as I watched her work behind the bar, I tried to figure out what it was about Wyn that made her different. Objectively, she wasn't the prettiest woman I'd ever seen, but she became the most beautiful woman in the world to me the longer I watched her. She wasn't the hottest, nor was she the sexiest. But, again, as the weeks passed one into the other, the more I got to know her, the more I noticed her above all others. She was sexy. She was hot. But even more than the superficial shit, she was real, she was giving, she was quirky and she was flawed. She wasn't a woman whose perfection demanded a pedestal; she was a very down-to-earth woman who I saw clearly, imperfections and all. And she seemed to love me despite all of my own massive failings. Elowyn wasn't a nameless, faceless body to control but a woman to care for, and, eventually, to love.

But as much as I loved her, I worried that the need for control, so far lying dormant, would someday rear its ugly head, so I warned her. Repeatedly. Tell her so she knows and maybe she'll still love you anyway. I never wanted to blindside her, never wanted her to wonder what had happened. So I assured her that if she chose to move ahead with me, she had to know this was a possibility, and I blamed it on the biker lifestyle because to tell her about what was really driving it -- my need for control -- I'd have to tell her about my fucked up childhood, and neither one of us talked about our pasts. Told her I'd be careful, I'd always come home to her and we wouldn't talk about it when it happened. To me, it was nothing worth talking about anyway because it was just a way to exert control. Like a smoker needing a hit of nicotine and stepping outside for a cigarette, that's all sex with the club girls was to me.

And then, after I regained my control, I went and sat in my room, wondering why I had to do what I did. Nothing felt right until I went home to Elowyn in the morning. She dispelled the emptiness and disgust that I brought on myself. And for a while, it'd be enough, but then I'd sense something in her and worry she was going to leave me, and if she did that, I didn't know how I'd function.

Funny enough, it was only when she took herself out of my life that it all snapped into focus: the control that I craved was nothing more than an illusion. Sex with ridiculous rules wasn't giving me control of jack shit. In effect, I'd thrown away what I had with Elowyn because of something that didn't even exist. I'd traded everything for nothing.

"No," I said out loud to her. Firmly. Regaining my footing. No. Elowyn had just announced that she'd left me and I was going to have to figure out how to handle it.

Her startled eyes met mine. "No? No what, Lachlan?"

I stepped toward her. "No, I'm not going to have to figure out how to handle it because we're not done."

"Oh, we are," she said. It wasn't mean, just a statement of fact, and I think I would have preferred mean. But Elowyn was rarely mean. "We have to be. I want someone to love me and only me. And you've spread yourself a bit thin in that area, Lach."

"I did. I did, and I'm sorry, but I'm not letting you go, Wyn. I'm not just going to walk away from you. I'm going to fix myself and fix us. I'm never going to fuck around on you again."

"How are you going to manage that now that we're apart when you couldn't manage that when we were together? You know the old expression too little, too late? That describes us perfectly."

"No," I said, as if repeating that one little word could bring us back together. "I'm going to work on myself and I'm going to work on us and I'm not giving up. I'm not, Elowyn."

"My decision isn't up for a vote," she said.

Her tone of finality would have scared me at one time, but I had a purpose and an objective now. "Not asking for a vote, Wyn. I'm telling you what's happening here. You're going to see that I can be different. That I can be loyal. That I can be faithful. That however you need to be loved, I'll love you that way."

"So why didn't you do this before if it's possible?"

"You know that expression you don't know what you've got until it's gone? That'd be me. Hanging on to control...that's fucking out the window. I'll accept that I have no control where you're concerned when it comes to letting you leave my life."

"Lachlan, we're done. Face it. Time of death...I don't even know when it was. Maybe the first time you cheated was the beginning of the end. Maybe it was Yomi. I guess, in the end, it doesn't even matter."

"It matters. It fucking matters, Elowyn. Everything about you matters and I'm sorry I didn't show you that before. Do you remember what you told me when you agreed to be my ol' lady, Wyn?"

Wyn gave me the side eye because there was a lot she'd told me back then.

"You told me you loved me because I wasn't perfect. You loved me because I didn't expect you to be perfect. And I didn't, sweetheart. I tucked your words in my pocket and carried them with me every day. I'm not perfect. I hurt you. You've never talked about it, and maybe someday you will, but I'd like to heal the hurt I caused you and whatever hurts you had from before me, way back as far as you want to go. And I'll figure out how to do it. We can both heal and then we'll be ready for each other. Next time, Wyn, next time you give me your heart, I'm not messing around with it. Never again."

She looked down for a minute, and I wondered if anything I'd said and promised had gotten through the walls she'd put up against me. Please.

When she looked back up, I saw the answer. No. The walls were up and being fortified with each passing second.

"It's time for you to go now, Lachlan."

I had two options. Argue with her, plead my case some more...or go. Do what she asked.

"OK, Wyn. Thanks for listening to me." I gently touched the tip of her nose with the tip of my index finger, our traditional goodbye following a kiss. She wasn't ready for a kiss, so I did the next best thing.

"I'll be in touch," I promised, then walked out her door. Doing that was counter to everything I wanted to do, but that was something I figured I'd need to get used to.

It was time I started approaching Elowyn in a completely different way. On the drive back to the clubhouse, I thought of all the ways I could do that.

I was a man with a plan to win back the woman he loved.

Chapter 10 (Lachlan): Irony

We had a rotating schedule in the guest room, as our MC called it. If someone was in the guest room, that didn't mean we needed to put clean sheets on the bed and hang fresh towels in the bathroom. It meant we needed to get ready to inflict some pain and hose down the evidence.

In reality, the guest room was an underground, cement cell that had a chair bolted to the floor in the middle of the room, a large hook in the ceiling and a hidden wall of your typical tools: crowbar, flame thrower, a huge assortment of knives, screwdriver, saws, hammers, bolt cutters and, of course, a hose next to an industrial size container of bleach.

Regardless of a person's position in the MC, all of us except Orion had to serve on the guest room rotation, three brothers per week. This was my week in here, and since our guest wasn't leaving here alive, we had the wall of tools exposed. That was terrifying enough, and many of our guests had made the mistake of thinking the wall was simply a flex, but they soon learned it wasn't.

Today's guest was brought to us by a technicality that got all charges against him dropped despite being guilty as hell. Guilty of some very serious, very nasty crimes. Crimes that Butcher refused to allow in his territory and would ensure a message was sent letting people know this.

"Did you see the game last night?" Prick asked as he shoved a rag in the terrified guy's mouth. The screams got tiresome after a while, so a long time ago, we'd just started stopping them before they could begin. Prick was the brother Butcher sent in when someone needed to die quietly in his sleep while at home, someone who was too important to simply disappear and never be heard from again. So, one hidden needle prick and the job was done.

"Lost a hundred bucks on it," I told him. " And I don't even like baseball."

"Shoulda talked to me. Woulda told you it was a bad bet."

"Yeah, next time I will. The first and only time I didn't check it out with you, I lost. Lesson learned."

And wasn't that the theme of my life lately? Lesson learned. I'd spent the last week since visiting Elowyn thinking, Googling certain phrases, reading and then thinking some more. I went to a couple of bookstores, made some purchases, bought some highlighters...and felt like I was in college again. Only this time, I was studying me and what made me into the person I was. The person who could do what I'd been doing, knowing it was hurting Elowyn.

Every day I would send her two texts. The first was to wish her a good morning and a good day. The second one I sent at night, and I texted her a quote from whichever book I'd been reading. Then after each quote, I ended the text with I love you.

She didn't respond to any of them. I could see they were delivered and they were read, but what she was thinking I had no clue. Maybe she wasn't thinking anything. Maybe she just wished I'd stop bothering her. I kept waiting for her to block me, to give me that final push out of her life, but she never did. So, reading that as a good sign, I continued sending my texts.

When Elowyn had told me I had to get used to living without her, I don't think I'd ever felt so out of control before, not even when things were at their most awful with my father. What I feared most in life had happened and losing Elowyn was the worst thing I could have imagined.

So why did you put it at risk? Why risk the woman you love for a woman who means nothing to you except as a way to exert your control?

Those questions stumped me, but I knew I needed to figure out the answers if I ever hoped to win her back. I knew I had to change my thinking and some of my actions. Not every part of me needed to change, but the part that needed control in certain areas -- the part that became more important than Elowyn -- had to undergo a complete change.

To start, I made a list of everything Elowyn had complimented me about over the years, and I labeled that side THE GOOD.

I like the way you hold me close.

I love the way you're gentle with me.

I admire the way you work so hard for us.

That had been a conversation early on when she'd first moved in with me. She'd come home late, after I was already at home and she'd thrown herself onto the couch next to me.

"What's wrong, Wyn?"

"I hate my job," she'd said. "My boss is the biggest asshole in the world and he's always on me, just trying to get me to mess up."

"Any reason you have to stay there?"

She'd shrugged. "I just can't stand the thought of having to look for another job yet again."

"Unless you want me to take care of your problem, you're either going to have to bite the bullet and look for one or put up with him."

"I know," she said, sounding so dejected. "And as much as I appreciate the offer, I don't want you to take care of him. I mean it, Lach."

We'd had variations on that conversation a number of times, until I made a different offer to her one day. It went against my nature to not wait for her boss in the parking lot and have a talk with him about the way things were going to be. Elowyn had warned me repeatedly against trying anything with him, and I was willing to respect that. For now. My line in the sand was if she ever came home in tears, at which point I'd find her boss and draw out some tears from him.

But one day she came home so upset, she was shaking with rage, so I pitched her an idea I'd been thinking about for a while.

"Quit," I told her. "And before you protest, listen. Quit, and then take some time off for yourself. You've been working since you were fourteen, and maybe you need a break to think about what you want and how you can get it so you don't have to be under these assholes all the time. Take your time, put out some feelers and see what pops.

I want you to find a job that you like, in a better situation, one that makes you happy."

"Lach, I've never not paid my own way."

"I've got it covered, Wyn. You know I can afford to support both of us."

"I know," she'd admitted. "But I feel like it's taking advantage."

"You didn't ask, sweetheart. I offered."

Then I made a list on the other side of the paper labeled THE BAD, and under it I listed the aspects of me that I knew had hurt her.

Looking at that list gave me a direction to focus on. A starting point to becoming a better man.

And what irony there was in that, I thought, as I applied the blow torch to our guest.

CHAPTER 11 (ELOWYN): STATUS QUO

I looked at the short letter in my hand and read it for the fourth time since I'd plucked it out of my mail box ten minutes ago. Had I ever received a letter before in my life? A real-live, hand-written letter? I didn't think people did that anymore. And that it was from Lachlan? Doubly rare. When we'd lived together, I got Post-it notes stuck to the refrigerator or the bathroom mirror saying Have a good day, I'll miss you, Can't wait to see you tonight or the ever popular You know I love you.

But this was a full-page of writing:

Wyn, what else would you put on THE BAD list? I'm trying to work on myself and this is what I have so far. I'm trying to fix all of the mistakes I've made in the past with you, so I'm asking for your input instead of me just assuming I got all the shit I've done to you on my list. (I'm afraid I forgot something.) Please let me know what else needs to be added.

THE BAD

1. Cheating to feel like I had control

2. Not listening to Elowyn

3. Fucking with her self-esteem

4. Not letting her talk about my cheating (maybe this is part of #2 on the list?)

5. Never trying to fix/stop my cheating

6. Expecting Elowyn to be OK with my cheating because I warned her from the start

7. Not stopping my cheating after I saw how much it hurt Elowyn (this could be rolled up with #5, maybe, but it seemed important enough to have its own number)

8. Trying to push her into marriage every year and making it about what I wanted instead of what she wanted

9. Not talking about my past

10. Not talking about her past

11. Not loving Elowyn the way she deserved

12. Telling her you know I love you instead of I love you

I love you, Wyn.

Lachlan

I placed the letter on the counter, and it sat there, watching me, I swear, while I made dinner. I put it in front of my dinner plate when I sat down to eat and read it again. It sat beside me on the couch while I watched some reality TV, it stayed with me while I brushed my teeth and washed and moisturized my face and it slept on my pillow next to me all night. In the morning, it was in the bathroom with me while I showered, and it was on the counter as I made some coffee and ate a yogurt before I left for work.

Apparently, I was officially in a relationship with Lachlan's letter now.

Less than a day old, and the letter was already getting dog-eared. I couldn't even tell you how many times I'd read it. Well, two hundred thirty-nine times, but who was counting? He hadn't sent me a quote from whatever self-help book he was reading last night, but he had sent me an I love you text before I fell asleep and he'd sent me a good morning, have a good day text before I showered.

For three days, that letter stayed with me every moment, and I read that list. Over and over and over again. The next night after I'd received the letter, I'd gotten the usual quote from a self-help book and an I love you text. We were back to normal.

Well, our new normal. Him reaching out and me not responding. It would have been easy to text him back. Six years with someone, five of which were serious, was a difficult dynamic to give up even if that dynamic had needed to change. His BAD list was horrible and I'd lived it with him, but if he had a GOOD list, I wondered if he had our talks on it. Although we didn't discuss the elephant in the room, having someone to share your day with was nice. Having someone ask a question and care about your answer was an amazing feeling, something I hadn't grown up with and had never experienced prior to Lachlan. And I'd wished we could have talked about our most important issue with the ease we talked about everything else.

A week after the letter arrived, there was a bulkier package in my mailbox, but I could see from the envelope it was Lachlan's handwriting.

When I opened it up over the kitchen table, a book fell out. A paperback, a used one from the looks of the creased spine, and I turned it over to read the title. Overcoming Your Childhood. There was a Post-it on the front.

Don't know about your childhood.

But I'd like to.

This helped me understand some things about myself.

I love you.

The book reminded me of the time I'd tried to get Lachlan to read a spy thriller that I'd just finished.

Not much of a reader, Wyn. About the only thing I read is financial reports and the accounting spreadsheets for the club businesses. It's not how I like to spend my time.

He didn't read. What Lachlan liked to do was work two-thousand piece puzzles while he had the TV on and I was on the couch reading. He wouldn't work one-thousand, five-hundred or three-thousand piece puzzles, only two-thousand piece puzzles. Why? No clue other than he said he found them challenging and two thousand was a nice, round number. Now he was reading self-help books, and extremely serious ones at that? I wondered how long he'd keep this up, or if this self-improvement regimen was like a New Year's diet resolution that was abandoned by January nineteenth.

That night, however, while cuddled on my couch, I picked up the book he'd sent and started thumbing through it. Lach was a high-lighter, that was certain. Each page had at least two sentences high-lighted, and some of them I recognized from the quotes he'd sent me in his texts.

Many of the highlighted sections hit home with me, so I turned back to the first page and began reading. Two hours later, I lifted my head and realized I needed to get to bed so I could open the store early to receive the latest shipment. Carefully marking my page, I left the book on my coffee table and got ready for bed.

I loved Thursdays at the store because we had a book club of older ladies come in, and they ordered tea, ate some goodies and discussed raunchy books.

"I still say he cheated," Roberta said. They were discussing My Double-Tongued Alien Lover by Gracelyn Matthewson. "He stuck that delicious tongue of his into the other captive girl's mouth right in front of the heroine."

"They weren't together yet, though," Gladys objected. "Not officially anyway. And he didn't know the human concept of monogamy. So when Crizzall threw the dinner plate at him, he stopped after the one kiss."

"Still," Velma said, "if he did it once, he could do it again. He definitely had enough tongue to go around."

Smiling as I moved around them, I dusted shelves, tweaked end caps, and planned next month's window displays.

"Give us our five-minute debate topic," they called to me. At the end of every session, they did a round-robin debate, where each of the five book club members got to speak for one minute on the topic of my choice. I was never sure how I got roped into providing a topic, but they always asked me for it.

"Let's see," I said. "Going with the alien tongue action on two women, today's topic is: can cheaters change?"

"I'll start!" Velma said. And they were off, talking heatedly, and loudly, about the subject. At the end of the debate, there were two votes in favor of cheaters being able to change and three against.

"And where do you stand on the subject?" Velma asked me.

Normally, I would have given a joking answer, but I actually responded seriously. "I don't know. It's a question I've been thinking about a lot lately, and I wish I knew the answer."

They came up to buy next week's book club selection -- The Duke's Lusty Loins by Cree Foster -- and I noticed Roberta lingered behind when the other four had left.

"To answer your question, a cheater can change if he, or she, decides to commit to change." She looked me in the eye. "I know. And if you ever want a sounding board, I'd be happy to listen."

She grabbed her bag, and with a wink, walked out of the store. For the next four weeks, Roberta lingered behind the others at the end of book club.

"Have you figured out an answer to your question yet?"

I hadn't and told her so, and she gave me a knowing smile before she left.

For his part, Lach continued with his daily morning and evening texts, never asking me to text back, just keeping in one-sided touch. I'd finished the first book he'd sent, and started on the second one that had arrived in the mail, The Control Myth. It was fascinating to me what he highlighted, and it began to give me more insight to the man.

Although I was building a new set of friends in my new town through work and my apartment complex get togethers, I still kept in touch with my old friends from the neighborhood, and to a very limited extent, the ol' ladies from the MC. My life was busy and full and I loved managing my own store. Me, the girl who would never amount to anything.

Life was steady and predictable, and if that was a bit boring, boring was sometimes OK for a time. I could add some excitement in when I felt ready for it. For now, status quo was satisfactory.

Until Lachlan changed things up with a new text one night:

Will you let me come see you?

CHAPTER 12 (ELOWYN): CONFRONTING AVOIDANCE

✱ ****TW for reference to domestic violence *****

I understand.

It was too soon to ask. I'm sorry.

I love you, Wyn.

That's all the tiny card said that came with the bouquet of flowers just delivered to the store. For Lachlan to send flowers was unusual. He was a more practical gesture kind of man. A brake job for my car. Washing my car every week and detailing it. Turning over a section of our backyard to create a vegetable garden for me because I mentioned I wanted to start one. Researching what vegetables you shouldn't grow together to help me lay out the seeds properly. Laying down a brick patio in the backyard because I'd mentioned wanting one.

Researching how to make a koi pond that I wanted and then finding all the different colors of koi he could.

Do you want a variety of colors or just go with the gold and white ones, Wyn?

In the time we'd been together, Lachlan had rarely veered from the practical. He'd given me three pieces of jewelry over five years, things he'd noticed me looking at when we'd been out but which had been too much money so I'd walked on by. They'd miraculously appeared on the kitchen table the next morning, not wrapped, in whatever box the jeweler had provided. Lachlan never held them back until my birthday or Christmas.

"My birthday's in six weeks," I'd protested when I'd opened the earrings. "We'll just call this an early birthday present."

"No, we won't," Lach had said. "You don't ask for anything."

I'd wanted to ask for something, but I was afraid he'd ask for something in return, and that I just couldn't do.

"This is why you never tie yourself to a man," my mother had told me, pointing to her swollen face and split lip. "So you can just take off if necessary."

Now he'd sent flowers in response to my turning him down when he asked if I would let him come visit.

"Pretty flowers," Roberta said to me, admiring the mixed bouquet of pink lilies and roses in the clear glass vase that I'd set on the checkout counter. Once again, Roberta had lingered behind the others at the end of book club, making sure she was always the last to buy the next week's book selection.

"Thank you," I said, admiring them right along with her.

"Did you find an answer to your question yet?"

She'd been asking for five weeks now, and I was no closer to an answer despite Lach's daily texts.

"Not really. No. I mean, how do you ever know if a cheater's actually changed?"

"That's a great question, and I wish I had an answer to it," she said thoughtfully. "I think it's similar to when no blood test exists to prove someone definitively has a disease and they have to go by the symptoms to make a diagnosis. You kind of have to look at a cheater and go by the signs to determine in what ways he's changed...or hasn't changed."

"I just don't know," I semi-whined.

"One of the hardest things in the world is to find out that your man is cheating on you. Your trust is destroyed and it takes a huge leap of faith to even think about trusting again."

Hmmm. "I knew," I admitted to her.

"Oh, Elowyn, I'm sure you did. I think women almost always know, deep down."

Could this get any more uncomfortable?

"No, I'm not talking about a gut feeling, Roberta. I mean we'd been seeing each other...and then right as we were talking about my becoming his ol' lady, he told me I needed to know that he'd occasionally cheat on me, but that I was the one he loved and he'd always come home to me."

That had surprised Roberta. It would probably surprise any rational, thinking woman.

"Oh, honey, what happened to you?" she asked softly, her eyes warm and sympathetic.

"I don't understand."

"What happened to you to make you accept that?"

Don't expect too much from a man. They all start out nice and then they turn on you.

As long as he's not hitting you, be happy with what he's willing to give you.

Leave yourself an out, Elowyn. Never tie yourself to him. Ever.

"I don't know how to answer that, Roberta," I said, trying not to sound as defensive as I felt. So I tossed the argument at her that I'd used on myself over the years. "Women marry men thinking they're going to be faithful because they promised to be -- only to find out they've been cheating. I knew from the start cheating was possible. Probable." I shrugged. "Which is the bigger betrayal? Promising to be faithful and then cheating or telling someone straight up, from the start that the cheating will happen?"

She tilted her head at me, trying to puzzle something out. "And could you cheat?"

"I could have, I suppose. Lachlan would have hated it, oh, he would have hated it, but he would have had no choice but to accept it or lose me."

"So did you?"

"No, because I didn't want to. I'd lost interest in multiple partners given my past. I'd been really...active from the time I was sixteen until even after I met Lachlan. And about a month after I met him, I just became really disgusted with myself one day. I wasn't having sex because I liked it all that much. I was just having it in the hopes that..."

"Someone would love you?"

"Not even love. I would have settled for affection. Caring. Any kind of concern." Pathetic, Elowyn.

"I see." And the way she said it made me think she really did get it.

"So your Lachlan didn't love you, but maybe he cared for you?"

"He said he loved me." Kind of. You know I love you. "But he started cheating after a year of me being his ol' lady, so maybe he didn't."

Some customers walked into the shop, chattering and laughing, and Roberta looked over her shoulder at them and then back at me. "I'd love to talk more next week, if you're willing."

I returned her smile because, despite being about forty years older than I was, she was easy to talk with. No judgment, just honest curiosity about my situation.

I didn't thank Lach for the flowers, which I suppose was bad manners but I wouldn't be maneuvered into having to contact him. The No I'd returned in answer to his text asking if he could visit was enough.

When I went home that night, I was thinking over my conversation with Roberta as I made a simple dinner of chicken salad, rolls and peas. This was comfort food for me, and for some reason, after the conversation with Roberta and after receiving the flowers, I needed comfort. I'd forced myself to leave the flowers at work because it was bad enough that I carried Lachlan's letter around with me still. By now, I had it memorized. All the words and items on his BAD list were committed to memory.

As I had dinner once again with Lachlan's letter, it gave me an idea based on something Roberta had said.

I think it's similar to when no blood test exists to prove someone definitively has a disease and they have to go by the symptoms to make a diagnosis. You kind of have to look at a cheater and go by the signs to determine in what ways he's changed...or hasn't changed.

So maybe I could diagnose Lachlan. Maybe I could determine if he was really trying to change or just trying to make me think he was to get me to come back home to him. Grabbing some paper, I put the header at the top: Signs Lachlan Is Trying to Change (At Least Himself And Maybe That Will Lead To Him Not Being A Cheater But It's Too Soon To Tell).

Well, that header was long as hell, but I started on the items in my list.

1. He opened up about his past to me/talked to me about his cheating

2. He's not trying to railroad me into coming back

3. He's recognized all the ways he hurt me and all the ways his cheating hurt me

4. He's reading self-help books to understand himself

5. He keeps reaching out to me despite never getting an answer from me

I pursed my lips, considering the list I'd created and compared it to his. Mine still wasn't definitive proof in the slightest. It still didn't mean anything had truly changed or he wouldn't revert to his old ways. It still didn't mean I could or would get over his cheating and his unwillingness to discuss it. It didn't mean I would ever be his one and only, and I refused to ever settle again.

Elowyn, if you find someone willing to provide a good home for you, take it. Don't expect perfection because it doesn't exist, especially not for someone like you.

My mother's words came back to me at odd times, as much as I tried to shut them out. While she hadn't been a terrible mother, she certainly hadn't been a nurturing one. Her calls had always frustrated me, and one day, when she'd said something so mean that it actually made me start crying, Lachlan grabbed the phone from me and practically snarled at my mother.

"You call her again, I'll find you and make it so you can't call her again. I don't know jack shit about you, lady, but you don't get to make her cry. She'll call you if she wants to talk to you."

Apparently, the irony of that conversation was lost on Lachlan at the time. That byplay was fresh in my mind the next day when I got my mail and there was a letter tucked into a book from Lachlan that he'd clearly read and marked up.

Confronting Avoidance

I couldn't wait to see what Mr. Avoidance himself had marked up in this book.

It would be illuminating.

CHAPTER 13 (LACHLAN): MAKING MY PLANS

I stood in front of Butcher's desk while those penetrating silver eyes examined me like I was a new species he'd discovered.

"Why?"

That was a damn good question he was asking me in response to the idea I'd just pitched to him. The honest answer might get me killed or squashed like a bug, but Butcher would know in a second if I was lying, so the truth it was.

"Because of Elowyn," I said slowly. "I don't want to leave the Mayhem, but I need to be near her."

"She left you."

Nodding, I couldn't deny it. "She did. She still doesn't want anything to do with me."

That made him tip his head to the side. "So you want to relocate to be near a woman who no longer wants to be with you."

I pointed to the financials I'd laid out in front of him and subtly corrected my president. "To scout the town as a potential place to begin a chapter of the Mayhem. I've done some preliminary research and the area has potential to be lucrative for us. Definite room for growth for us. The town lost two major factories, businesses were closing. Some revitalization has already begun, but we could pretty much take over the town, open some businesses, employ the people who lost jobs and haven't been able to move away."

His eyes flicked to the papers then back to me. "All this for some woman."

"No. All of this for Elowyn, not some woman. It made sense to me as I was thinking about my situation. We've got a lot of brothers now and the MC is huge. I need to be near her and a chapter makes financial sense for the MC."

"Find another woman."

"I don't want to."

"Why the hell not?"

"Because I love her."

"You love a woman who left you."

This was new territory for me, talking about a woman with him. Butcher normally had no patience with or interest in our personal lives -- until they interfered with our MC lives. And then he'd come down on you like a ton of bricks for putting someone ahead of the MC. But lately, since we'd had a certain woman as an overnight guest, he'd been off.

Had it been anyone else, I would have said distracted, but Butcher never wavered as head of the MC. His focus was absolute and intense.

"Yeah. I love Wyn."

"How do you know?"

At his question, I almost choked. "How do I know I love her?"

He just stared at me, unwilling to repeat his question and waiting for an answer. My brain was stumbling around, trying to figure out how to describe love to a man who only became somewhat talkative or animated when he was about to torture or take apart an enemy.

Fuck. He wouldn't get any of this, but when Butcher wanted an answer, you gave him an answer.

"I think about her all the time. She's never far from my thoughts. When I'm with her, I feel good inside, like everything's right. When I'm not with her, I can't wait to be with her again. I like hearing the sound of her voice, I want to take care of her and --"

Still nothing on his face, so I went for it.

"And every time I see her face, it's like that feeling you get when you're on your bike, going full throttle down the road and you feel like you're flying."

"She left because you cheated on her repeatedly."

I wasn't surprised he knew that. Butcher might not like to discuss anything personal, or even admit the brothers had lives outside of the MC, but he sure as fuck knew the last little details of what was happening in our lives.

"She did. I'd been hurting her for years with my cheating."

"So forget about her."

"I can't. I'm working on being a stronger man, and all I want to do is make it up to her. Fix it. Be better. Show her I'm working on myself and I won't hurt her anymore."

"Seems like a lot of trouble for a female."

Like having two brothers watch over a certain female twenty-four/seven?

Instead of allowing that death sentence to come out of my mouth, I agreed. "Maybe it is. But she's worth it."

"You have two months," he said suddenly. "And you know what'll happen if you're dicking around with her and not scouting the area thoroughly. We'll take it to church tomorrow and get the votes, then at the end of the week, you'll head out with Orion for two months. If things look like this will be a lucrative and strategic move, we'll go ahead with a chapter."

"I won't let you down, Butcher."

The idea passed in church, and as soon as it was approved, that night I sent a text to Elowyn, wondering what she'd think.

I just want you to know that I'll be in the area starting Saturday for the next two months.

Nothing back from her. Not for three days. Then: Why?

Club business. Two towns over from yours.

I still don't want to see you.

Yet. You still don't want to see me yet, my brain filled in because I couldn't imagine my life without her, so defeat was not an agony I was willing to accept. But now that I wasn't going to be so far away from her, I hoped that I could convince her to see me, to let me try to make it up to her, to talk with me.

I'd watched her slipping away from me but I kept reminding myself that she'd known what she was getting into with me. I'd been up front from the start, just not up front about the details of why or what my stupidity involved. I'd stubbornly continued on my path of destruction, refusing to discuss it with her when she brought it up because I was a coward, clinging to the but you agreed to it defense that turned out to be nothing but an admission of guilt and my sentence was losing Elowyn. She'd had to escape from our relationship because I hadn't done right by her.

Orion and I headed out early on Saturday morning. We were both looking forward to the trip for different reasons. He'd never admit it, but he was running from something, while I was running toward something. Hoped I was running toward something, anyway. Two months wasn't a lot of time with a woman I'd wronged so badly, but I was determined to win her back.

As we rode, my brain was already working on two different missions, MC and personal. Performing due diligence on the town and winning back Elowyn. As a Mayhem brother, I knew what my prime objective should be, but as a man who'd lost the woman I loved because of my refusal to stop hurting her due to my own issues, that was my primary goal.

The ride was easy and we had good weather as we took off, which I hoped was a good omen. Cresting a hill, we saw the road ahead of us and Orion looked over at me, grinning. I grinned back and we both settled in to enjoy the long ride. With every mile forward, Orion was that much farther away from his troubles, and I was that much closer to mine.

We pulled up to the extended stay hotel we'd booked for the next two months and checked in. After hitting a nearby bar for some food and a beer, we headed back and went to our bedrooms. Tomorrow, Orion and I would talk about strategies for scouting the town.

But tonight was for thinking about Elowyn and making my plans. After a couple of hours of her face in front of me, I sent her my good night text.

In Pineville. Sleep well. I love you.

She didn't answer.

CHAPTER 14 (ELOWYN): THE NEW PARTS

Following book club, Roberta, as usual, maneuvered herself to the end of the line so she'd be the last one buying next week's book selection.

"How are you doing on your attempt to find an answer about cheaters?" she asked me, her smile kind and interested as I rang up her purchase.

"He's in the area. For the next two months." I avoided answering Roberta, but I spilled some interesting tea for her. Fair trade, I supposed.

"Will you see him?"

"No," I said definitively as I popped her book into a bag.

Roberta watched my face, not saying anything.

"Probably not," I amended my first response.

She nodded.

"I doubt it."

Shut up, Elowyn!

"Maybe?"

She continued watching me without uttering one single word. Saying nothing seems so passive, but really it's quite aggressive. It's an in-your-face flex that keeps the conversational ball squarely in the other person's court.

"What would be the purpose?" I asked desperately after a tiny staring contest where I blinked first. I handed her bag and receipt over to her.

"That is an excellent question, Elowyn."

"Should I, do you think? See him?"

"Why would you?"

Dammit. Roberta was good at returning a question for a question. I didn't exactly like it because I wanted her to tell me what to do since she obviously had experience with a cheater. Cheaters? I wanted to benefit from her experiences, have her tell me definitively what to do so I didn't have to hold all of the internal debates I'd been having since Lach had texted me that he was going to be nearby for the next two months.

I still don't want to see you.

That hadn't been the complete truth when I'd texted him that, but I felt like I needed to make a strong statement back to him so he wouldn't think I was wavering, which...I was. It was the response I knew I should give, a show of force. But part of me did want to see him, see this man who was such a mess inside but was trying to work on himself. You're just as big a mess, Elowyn, but what have you done to help yourself?

When I didn't have an answer at the ready, Roberta leaned in a bit. "Maybe that's an easier question to ponder this week than the bigger one you've been thinking about. Sometimes it helps to break down those seemingly overwhelming questions into smaller, bite-sized pieces." She lifted her bag containing the novel for next week's book club discussion and rolled her eyes. "I'll try to get through My Secret Lover's Dark Secret while you work on figuring out an answer."

As ordered, I tried to answer the question, trying out different variations. Why would I see Lachlan? Why would I see Lachlan? Why would I see Lachlan? No matter how I asked it, I couldn't come up with a good reason that made me want to text him back with an answer one way or the other. That was the fear controlling me. Fear that, deep down, I wanted to see him.

In addition to the daily good morning and good night texts he continued to send, Lach texted me a couple of times throughout the day, pictures of gardens he saw or just pretty landscapes. He still sent quotes from whatever self-help book he was reading, and when he finished the book, he sent it on to me. Based on the book titles, the sheer number of book titles and the amount of underlining he was doing, he was working hard to understand himself, what was driving him and how his past had helped define his present. There were books about breaking free of the past's ties and carving out a new future for yourself that wasn't controlled by childhood issues and traumas.

Why would you see him?

There were only a couple of reasons. To say hello to someone I shared a life with for so long. To give him a strong message to stay out of my life. To see why he was in town. To see if he was still the same man who'd cheated on me.

A week after he texted me that he was in town, a box of cupcakes from my favorite bakery were delivered to my store with a note.

Wyn, I'm sending this instead of texting to put less pressure on you. If you'd be willing to meet, have coffee, share a meal, anything, just text me a time and place and I'll be there. I'll understand if you say no.

Him and his damn no pressure and understanding. The Lachlan I knew wasn't like that. I thought about his request as I ate the dozen cupcakes over the next two days, practically making myself sick on the rich icing and fillings. (Totally worth it, by the way.) I thought about the question Roberta left me with. I thought about all of the hurt inside of me, some of it caused by his actions, some of it caused by my passivity, and some of it caused by the uncertainty churning inside me.

In desperation, I called Roberta. She'd given me her number a while back, but I hadn't yet used it.

"Tell me what to do. He sent cupcakes and asked to see me. And...I'm seriously considering it. Talk me out of it."

"I can't tell you what to do."

"You have to have an opinion!"

"Your opinion is the only one that matters here, Elowyn. You need to make this decision by yourself and for yourself. No one else."

"I know." Dejection had a sound, and it caught in my voice.

She hesitated when she heard my breath hitch. "Ask yourself who you're going to be meeting. The old Lachlan or the new Lachlan? Do you want to meet either one? Or is he now just someone you once loved no matter who he is today?"

The next day, after a sleepless night thinking about Roberta's never-ending questions, I sent a simple text to Lachlan: Cello's at 7 pm Thursday

His response was immediate. Meet you there or pick you up?

Meet you there

Thank you, Wyn

I arrived at the restaurant just after seven, having been held up a few minutes at work balancing the day's receipts. Lachlan was already there in black jeans, black boots, black Henley and cut. I watched him watch me, taking me in from head to toe.

"You look great, Wyn," he said sincerely. "Beautiful."

I could tell he wanted to hug me, but he held himself back.

"They don't do reservations, so we might have a wait," I said. "They're always busy."

"We don't have to wait," he said, then held the door open for me so I could enter the restaurant. When we stepped up to the hostess stand, he said, "We're ready to be seated."

The hostess snapped to and gave us a welcoming smile as she grabbed two menus. "Right this way, please."

She walked us to a table near the stone fireplace, and he held my chair out and then sat across from me. A server took our drink orders, and I kept shooting glances at him to find his eyes steadily on me.

Lach kept the conversation light, and although I'd been tense at first, I slowly relaxed and we talked the way we used to through our appetizers, meals and desserts. It was both familiar and new at the same time, but surprisingly comfortable most of all.

He'd surprised me when he told me he and a brother were scouting the area as a possible location to begin a charter of the Lords of Mayhem.

"I'm thinking the area wasn't random?"

"No. Not in the slightest," Lach admitted. "Told Butcher I didn't want to leave Mayhem, but I would if needed so I could live near you. And then I pitched my idea of a charter to him out here. The Mayhem's gotten huge in the last few years, so it makes sense to branch out."

As we were lingering over coffee, Lachlan leaned across the table toward me, his eyes searching mine.

"Elowyn, I destroyed us. We talked about it when I came out here before."

I nodded.

"And I've been thinking about nothing else but how to make this right between us. So I began working on myself, learning about all the shit inside me, looking deep into things I never wanted to think about again. But I was more than willing to if it meant working through them and understanding how they affected me so I could come back to you a better man."

I knew Lachlan and knew talking about this wasn't easy. He'd never wanted to have difficult discussions before, never would have admitted to his struggles like this. And neither did you, Elowyn. You held back, didn't push, accepted.

His hand covered mine. "I broke what we had between us and hurt you so bad you left. But I've been wondering, Wyn, if you think there are enough pieces of us left to put back together. To make something whole from, and we could fill in any gaps with the new parts of ourselves."

CHAPTER 15 (ELOWYN): YOU'RE NOT ALONE

"Lach," I said, "if there's one thing that's become clear to me, it's that we were toxic together. I don't see how we go back to that or even why we'd want to."

"Two things. First, the way we were was toxic. The way we were. No doubt, Elowyn. I'm working on straightening myself out, but it's going to take work because I'm seriously fucked up. That's the reason I send you the books I'm reading, so you can see what I'm learning and figuring out about myself. So you can see I'm one hundred percent serious about not being a total fuck up anymore and hurting you ever again."

Reaching across the table, his scarred, thick fingers drew patterns on the back of my hand.

"If you figure out what the problem is, if you figure out what's wrong with you, you can learn from your mistakes and be better by fixing yourself. I wanted to fix myself for you, Wyn, for us. Reading these fucking books -- it's like the authors are talking right to me, like they know exactly what I went through growing up. I'm working on myself so that when you're ready to come back to me, you'll know you're safe, and I won't ever hurt you again."

"That's a lot of work with no guarantee that I'll come back to you in the end."

"Not going to lie, Wyn. I started this because I knew it was the only chance I had to get you back. But as I've gotten more into it, whether or not you come back to me, I need to do this, see it through. For me. I'm fixing me for me and for you. Didn't like myself for what I did to you, but when I thought about it more, I also just plain didn't like myself. And I especially didn't like myself because what I did hurt you and drove you away, and I had to live my life without you. Well, Wyn, living without you is hell on earth. So I made up my mind that I'm not going to live without you if I can help it, and I'm learning that I can help it. I'm going to earn you back. And the first step is me."

All of this was coming from a man who never wanted to talk about deep emotions. He was the kind of man who didn't spend time on self reflection, feelings and emotions. Lachlan was goal-oriented, task-driven, straightforward and unswerving with a focus on getting the job done and done well.

"I'm looking at it like I want to go pick you up for a date, Elowyn, but I go out to my bike and it's broken down. Can't pick you up 'til the bike's fixed, so job one is fixing the damn bike."

He was so earnest it broke my heart, my heart that had already been broken by him in a much different way. Lachlan, from the first time I met him, was always confident, a stoic badass, a tower of strength. Now, I was being given a glimpse of the little lost boy he carried inside peeking through his rough features. This man was riddled with scars inside and out, but his determination to be more than he had been was almost palpable.

"And the second thing?" I asked, watching his fingers on mine.

"The second thing is I'm going to remind you about the good parts of us. The good things, the right things, and there were good things despite all the bad things I did. There were ways we were strong. Those are the pieces I'm talking about fitting together again."

I needed to think about what he'd just said later, when I was alone and had time to really pick it apart and examine his words for flaws and truths.

"One of the things I've been learning is to look at myself realistically and not to apply absolutes. It's really easy to say I'm a total piece of shit person and there's nothing good about me and to leave it at that. People throw up their hands in a fight and say well, guess I'm just an asshole then! But that's the easy answer, the cop out to avoid trying to improve yourself. I'm saying guess I'm just an asshole...but I don't want to be one so now I'm going to fix that. Unless you're a complete psychopath, and I know a few of those, there are parts of everyone that are good. So what I'm learning is to look at the good and the bad in myself and work to understand why I have those bad parts and what I can do to repair those. But the other half of that shit is to look at the good parts of me and work to make those even stronger. It's playing to your strengths."

I didn't need to think about that for even a second to realize that he spoke an important truth. Condemning someone wholly and across the board wasn't valid for the most part. It was a basic fact of life: good people did bad things and bad people did good things. It was our nature. I thought back to those nights years ago when Lach had stationed himself nearby while I was in the alley with one of the men from the bar where I worked. Lachlan was the first man who'd ever looked out for me without expecting something in return, and I remember being surprised when he hadn't treated me like a slut.

He could have. He definitely could have and I wouldn't have blinked an eye because that was how I saw myself. Lachlan still had no clue how many men I'd been with before him, why I'd been with so many, what made me use men to try to fill up the missing pieces and gaps inside me.

If I was going to be honest with myself, Lachlan hadn't been the only broken one in our relationship. He was, however, the only one seriously trying to fix himself. Even though I'd finally gathered the courage, self-respect and reserves to leave him, I hadn't tried to fix myself, to address the reasons I'd been willing to accept much less than I should have. I'd simply changed locations after deciding I'd had enough, dragging my baggage and old habits with me, but I hadn't truly looked within myself the way Lach was in the process of doing.

My mind flashed back to a conversation I'd had with Roberta when I'd told her I'd gone into a relationship with Lachlan knowing he'd cheat on me.

Oh, honey, what happened to you?

I don't understand.

What happened to you to make you accept that?

It was a simple yet complicated answer that I didn't like to think about: my mother had happened to me. The way I'd grown up had happened to me. My pain had happened to me.

I twisted my hands so they took ahold of Lachlan's hands. Those strong, square hands that were battered and scarred.

Like the two of us were.

And even still, the feel of them, the familiar roughness, the sheer strength brought me comfort.

"I'm...I don't know the right word, here, Lach -- impressed? glad? awed? -- that you're working on yourself and making changes. But listening to you has made me realize that I need to work on myself."

His eyes were watching me carefully, beautiful in their steadiness.

"I've been reading the books you've been sending me, looking at what you've been highlighting. And you've been really brave because the sentences or paragraphs you're highlighting are excruciating, Lach. They're really hard to apply to myself because they open old hurts, make me think about things I've never wanted to revisit. But I've been thinking, with every book you send, that I need to start the same journey you did. And I don't know if I can make any promises --"

His hands squeezed mine as I choked.

"Elowyn, I get it. I know what you're saying," that rough voice was choked, too. "You need time. I won't push you because it's hard. You're the only one who knows what I'm doing, and sending you texts every day helps ground me and makes me feel like I'm not so fucking alone. Got all the brothers in the world, but you're the only one I can share shit with. Taking a look at yourself is going to hurt, so I'll make the offer of being your friend with no other expectations."

He swallowed, his jaw ticking.

"But promise me something, Wyn. Those days when it gets to be too fucking much because there's that much pain coming out of you, reach out to me, even if it's just to cry. I'll sit with you and not say a word. I'll be on the other end of the phone and listen. I'll walk with you while you clear your heart. Whatever you need, ask. I'm not afraid to talk anymore, and I just want you to know while you work through things that you're not alone."

CHAPTER 16 (ELOWYN): I CAN HELP

✱ **TW for mentions of child abuse***

Lachlan had followed me home after we finished dinner and talking, and he walked me to my door.

"Thank you for tonight, Wyn. I know it can't be easy to see me so it makes me appreciate your willingness to meet me even more."

He'd been brutally honest all night, so I thought I'd return the favor and give him a glimpse into me, a specific one I'd never been willing to give him before when we were together.

"It's not easy...and it is. I'm tempted every day to go back to you and sweep what you did under the rug because at least you never hit me or threw things at me or broke my arms or ribs."

Although he tried not to react, my confession electrified Lach and he seemed to grow before my eyes, his face furious.

"Elowyn." Agony in those three syllables.

And then he stepped to me, his arms wrapping protectively around me, my ear pressed to his chest.

"I'm so sorry, Wyn. So damn sorry."

What he was sorry for exactly, he didn't say. It sounded like he was apologizing both for what I'd witnessed and experienced as a child and for cheating on me when we'd been together.

But he continued.

"I'm sorry for adding to your pain. I'm sorry I didn't stop hurting you when I could see how much pain I was causing you. I'm sorry we talked about every damn subject under the sun except the most important ones -- our fucking pasts."

Even though his arms around me felt so good, felt like home, I stepped out of his hold and he loosened his arms immediately, letting me go. His eyes, though, his eyes were darkened with pain for me.

"It's ironic," I said to him. "How easily we could talk about anything and everything but neither of us was willing to discuss how we grew up."

"Told you tonight I'm not afraid to talk about things anymore. You got a question, I'll answer it. You want to know something, I'll tell you. I know to have a hope in hell of getting you back in my life, I can't hide shit anymore and I don't want to. It's total shit, but it's part of me, and you need to know about where I came from and the reasons behind why I did what I did. Not saying the reasons excuse it but that understanding has been helpful to me so I can start to correct shit."

"I think I'd like to get to that understanding myself. I know what you're doing isn't easy or fun, so I think what you're doing takes guts."

"It ain't easy, that's for sure," Lach said. "I'd like to see you again in a few days. Hell, I'd like to see you tomorrow and the next day and all the rest of my days, but I think I should back off for a few days. Let it all sink in."

"I think that's best, too, Lach."

"Then I'll spend the next few days focused on club business, which'll make Butcher happy."

"He does happy?" I looked skeptically at Lach. His MC president was the scariest man I'd ever seen and in all the years that I'd been in his vicinity, I'd never seen him smile.

"OK. Yeah. That might be a stretch. Maybe it will make Butcher less homicidal than normal?"

I laughed because he wasn't wrong, and since it was always good to end a night with laughter, I told Lachlan good night and went into my place. Going to my front window, I listened for the loud thunder of Lach's Harley, and when I heard it rumble to life, I peeked out my curtain and watched him ride away.

Then I threw myself down on my couch and went over the evening.

I'm going to remind you about the good parts of us. The good things, the right things, and there were good things despite all the bad things I did. There were ways we were strong. Those are the pieces I'm talking about fitting together again.

As much as I didn't want to admit it, Lach had been right. It sounded ridiculous to say that other than that nasty cheating habit of his, we had a good relationship. I wasn't sure if that was valid. Did the cheating negate everything we had? I'd need to talk to Roberta since she'd been cheated on before and seemed to have a realistic view of life.

I thought of the way Lachlan and I had talked every day. Sometimes the conversations were basic, handling details like what to make for dinner and bills and things on the calendar. But most of the time, we talked about everything imaginable. Funny things we'd heard that day, things we'd seen, current events, local politics, neighborhood happenings, movies we'd seen, TV shows we were enjoying. And although he was nowhere near as social as I was, he loaned muscle when needed for our neighborhood block parties, he'd man the grill or act as bartender. Sometimes, he'd take on all three for one event if we were short on help.

"You say you hate socializing, but you're always at the block parties," I'd teased him.

"Because you are," he'd explained as if it were the most obvious thing. "You want to go be social, have time with your girls, I'll go with you and talk with the other men. It's not my favorite thing, but you are, so I go."

Unwilling to think about the other things we'd shared, I decided to put the rest on hold and ask Roberta when I saw her in a few days.

This week, I'd been impatient for book club to be over. The ladies' banter and obscene comments didn't make me smile to myself this week like they always did. I didn't want to give them a five minute discussion topic at the end. I wanted to order everyone out so I could talk with Roberta.

At long last, the book club members filed out, new books in hand, and Roberta was the last one to make her purchase.

"Roberta, can I ask you something?" I asked after I put her book in a bag.

Her smile was sweet. "Absolutely."

"So I apologize in advance if what I'm about to say brings up some old pain, but I wonder, when you got cheated on, did that mean everything about your relationship was a lie? That it couldn't have had anything good about it because the cheating overshadowed everything else?"

She gave me a strange look before speaking. "Let me ask you this, Elowyn. You knew he was cheating. He wasn't hiding it. And you stayed, for a long time. Did it feel as if every moment was a lie?"

"No, not every moment. Maybe they started to in the end when he was cheating more often. Did you feel that way?"

"I'm curious why you think I've been cheated on."

"You told me," I answered.

To answer your question, a cheater can change if he, or she, decides to commit to change. I know. And if you ever want a sounding board, I'd be happy to listen.

"Oh, I can see where I wasn't clear," Roberta said, "I was talking about my experience with several couples who had faced infidelity. I've been with them through the worst of it."

"And did their relationships survive it?"

"Some of them did," Roberta said. "And that's because they fought hard for it. And they wouldn't have fought, Elowyn, if they felt their whole relationship was a lie. They wouldn't have fought if they didn't think there was something to salvage from the wreckage."

"No, I guess there'd be no purpose to fighting if they didn't have anything real to save."

"Exactly. You only try to save those relationships with people you love."

"Lachlan and I had a good talk when we went out the other night," I explained to her. "And we both agreed that just like he's working on himself, I need to look at all that's broken in me and glue it back together so I don't make the same mistake again. So I stop hurting myself. Until I do that, there's no point in even trying to have a relationship with any man. I just need to look deep inside and fix myself."

"I think we were meant to meet," Roberta said, "because I can help you with that."

CHaPTer 17 (LacHLan): A BOOK STore

Used to be, the hardest thing in my life was determining which tool to use on someone we wanted to talk. Cause too much pain, they won't be able to talk; too little pain, and they don't take you seriously and can withhold information. Probably why Butcher had all of us take college-level anatomy courses so we could inflict maximum damage

Now, I had a list of the hardest things in my life.

Living with the knowledge that I hurt Wyn.

This one zipped-tied me to the chair in our MC's guest room on a daily basis and drilled holes directly into my heart. I saw it in her eyes. And her eyes told me she wasn't happy and that meant she'd probably bolt. Didn't know she was already working her escape plan. If I hadn't been such a coward, I could have faced what I was doing.

Living with the knowledge that Wyn carried the hurt I inflicted on her all the time.

Every time I thought about this one, I wanted to punch myself in the face. Wyn shouldn't be carrying this hurt with her because I was a weak asshole, but it was exactly what had happened. For years, I'd hurt her because something was wrong with me that bled out onto her and scored her deep.

Living with the knowledge that I wouldn't talk about my cheating with her.

That one? That was one of the most fucked things there was. After I told her I'd cheat and she was still willing to get official, that meant she was agreeing to the terms. When she tried to talk about it, I had to shut that shit down because it meant I would either have to walk away from her, and I didn't see how in the hell I could live without my Wyn, or I had to stop cheating. At that point, I didn't understand the need driving me; all I knew was I felt compelled to do it and didn't understand that there was actually something wrong inside me and there were strategies I could use to control it. So the obvious answer was to stop any and all attempts she made to talk about it. Period. Fucking genius move. Insert motherfucking eyeroll.

Living without Elowyn.

This sucked in too many ways to count. Every aspect of my life was dull. I didn't care about anything but improving myself and becoming a man who could win her back. Life without Wyn was like a life without air.

"Hey, brother," Orion came up, interrupting my thoughts, and sat on the bar stool next to me and signaled for a beer from the bartender.

I tipped my bottle to my lips and took a long swallow. "Hey," I said.

"You see Wyn?"

He and Butcher were the only ones who knew that the main reason I wanted to see if a chapter of the Mayhem would work here was Wyn.

"Not since last week," I said trying not to sound like a sad little bitch.

Last week when she'd opened up a little about her childhood, I'd wanted to burn the earth to the ground. Mother, with Butcher's approval, was working on some things for me, so we'd see if he could unearth anything. If anyone could, it'd be Mother. That bastard had skills, and I needed him so I could go on a hunt. So far, he'd gotten me Wyn's medical records and shared them with Butcher and me. That sort of shit didn't fly with any of us, and that was why Butcher had given the go-ahead for the deeper dive that would provide names and addresses.

After the bartender shoved her shoulders back so we'd notice her tits and slid Orion's beer in front of him, I told her to beat it until we wanted another round. She gave us a disgruntled look but walked away to help some customers at the other end of the bar. Everyone was giving Orion and me -- and our Mayhem cuts -- a wide berth.

We were hard to miss. Orion was as tall and wide as I was, maybe a little taller, but we all teased him about being a pretty boy because where my face looked like it been sculpted in stone using nothing but a hammer, Orion looked like one of those statues. Some rando had come up and hit on him in front of a lot of us one night when we were on a run and said he was beautiful, like the statue of David.

That had all of us whipping out our phones and Googling that shit if we'd missed it in our college art appreciation classes.

"This statue guy's barely got any dick," Trap howled. "She saying you're a dickless wonder, O?"

"Agreed, man. I'd be fucking sad if my dick was that scrawny looking," Mother had laughed.

After that, one of the brothers had ordered a small statute of David and set it up on the bar at the Mayhem clubhouse where it stayed until Butcher saw it and told us to get rid of the naked fucker.

"You think Butcher's going to go for a new chapter here? Potential seems good."

I thought about Orion's question. "Hope so. I think it'd be lucrative, and I need it to work here."

"What if he says no?"

I shrugged. "I leave the club. Move here to be near Wyn."

"You'd really quit?"

"Only for Wyn, but yeah, I'd quit for her."

"What if he gives the green light, you move here and she doesn't get back with you?"

"Haven't thought that far ahead yet. Can't think of a life without Elowyn. What about you?" I asked him. "If we set up a chapter here, you bringing your family or staying back there?"

That was a sore subject with Orion. He finished his undercover work and discovered he had a seven-year-old child and his old lady had just found out she was pregnant. He'd cut Kadie loose right before she told him, but it didn't matter to him that she was having his child. She'd unknowingly helped sell his undercover position as a biker and when his cover had been blown, he had no more use for her, pregnant or not.

So he said. When Butcher sent him on this run to check out the area, he'd left Elijah in the care of two club girls, paying them to watch his boy. Kadie had taken off and even Mother couldn't find her.

"Only got the kid," Orion said. "And I don't even want him."

We brothers were live and let live. Straight up. Didn't interfere in one another's personal lives. All we cared about was the club business getting done, being handled. Beyond that, unless the home life interfered with that, we never said shit.

But that pissed me the fuck off.

"Doesn't matter if you want him or not," I said, remembering how it felt to feel like I was in the way of my father's life. Unwanted. "I'll fucking knock your head off you ever say shit like that again."

I turned on my bar stool to face him fully. He was glaring at me as I went on.

"You don't want him, but you got him, asshole. He ain't some thing. He's a little kid who not too long ago lost his mom. You're all he's got and I don't give a damn you don't want him -- you fucking step up, fucking man up and see to him."

"Yeah, thanks for the advice, Shadow. That's rich coming from a man who fucked around on his old lady so bad that she took off and ghosted you. Tell me how to handle my shit when you can't even handle some bitch."

I didn't even think. Quick as I could, I grabbed his hair and smashed his face into the bar, probably breaking his nose.

"Call Wyn a bitch again," I dared him, still holding his hair in my fist.

The bartender flew over to us as I pulled Orion's head back and he swung out wildly, his nose bleeding badly. She had not one thought of flashing us her tits this time when she stopped in front of us.

"Take it outside," she snapped.

Releasing Orion, I stepped back, pulled my wallet and threw down a hundred dollar bill.

"Apologies."

Then I added another hundred.

"For your troubles," I explained.

I added one last hundred and inclined my head toward Orion.

"That's from him, with his apologies."

With that handled, we walked out of the bar, Orion holding his riding bandana to his nose. We stood by our bikes for a minute, while he tried to stop his nose bleeding.

"Don't know shit about being a father," he said quietly after a minute. "Never thought about being one."

"Don't know shit about being a good man," I returned, a little hesitant to keep going because this wasn't the kind of shit any of us talked about. "But I'm trying my best. Reading a shit ton of books to help, watching videos, listening to podcasts. Doing my best to be better, to be someone Elowyn deserves. I'm sure they got books to help clueless assholes who suddenly become fathers, too."

Orion looked away. "Books?"

"Yeah, they're these things with words on pages."

"Fuck off, asshole," he said, still mopping up his nose. "Is there a book store around here?"

"Yeah, I just happen to know where one is."

Chapter 18 (Lachlan): The Looks in Their Eyes

The only time I'd set foot in Elowyn's store before, I'd been too damn focused on Wyn to really take in the details of the place. I'd just scanned it for threats and then locked onto Wyn and kept my eyes on her.

Today, as Orion and I pushed through the glass door with the curly writing of the store name -- Sweet Reads -- on it, I noticed a soft series of chimes that announced our arrival. Kind of felt like a little AC/DC would have been more appropriate for the two of us coming into this place, but whatever.

The walls of the store were painted a pale yellow, and all the rows and rows of bookshelves were painted white. In the center of the store was a long display case, and at the far right was a sleek Point of Sale cash register. Everything to the left was bakery items, and even though I wasn't much for sweets, they looked good to me. Behind the display case was a long counter where the coffee shit happened with a couple of complicated, copper and brass machines. A younger woman stood behind the counter, purple haired and wearing a white apron with the store name on it.

Off to the side when you walked in was a seating area with two worn-leather couches facing each other and two overstuffed chairs at each end. An old, wooden industrial cart with cast iron wheels served as a coffee table. A bright bouquet of flowers was the only decoration on the coffee table.

Didn't know if Wyn had decorated the place, but it looked cozy and comfortable, just like she'd made our home. There were plants all over the store, and that definitely screamed Elowyn to me. My girl liked her greenery.

The seating area was currently filled with five older ladies who had their eyes glued to us. Orion looked over at the ladies with their jaws dropped, some frozen in the act of sipping coffee from their fancy china cups.

"If one of those bitches calls the cops on us, I ain't gonna be happy," Orion said to me quietly.

We would come to wish they'd been contemplating calling the cops on us.

Elowyn came around the end of one of the book shelves, carrying a small stack of books.

"Hello!" she greeted before we were fully in her view, then, when she saw who her latest customers were, her steps stuttered for a minute. It didn't take her long to regroup, and she walked toward us.

"Oh. Hey, Lachlan, Orion." She was trying hard not to stare at Orion's two black eyes and swollen nose.

"Lachlan?" I heard from one of the ladies.

"You know these boys, El?" one of the other ladies said.

I cringed, knowing that El was a shortened version of her name Elowyn didn't like very much. There was something in the lady's voice that, if I had to guess, wasn't fear but excitement. That surprised me since people usually weren't happy to see us.

"Yes, Velma," Wyn said. "These are some old acquaintances of mine."

That seemed to be a cue for all of the women to get up and rush over to us.

"Well, in-tro-duce us, please," one woman said and, without waiting, beamed up at Orion and me. "I'm Gladys," she practically cooed, while she blinked rapidly at us. "And aren't you just gorgeous. Mmmhmmm."

"Please, no," Elowyn murmured.

"The fuck?" Orion said to Gladys. "You got a problem with your eyes?"

"Hel-loooo, boys! This is so exciting to meet you. I'm Velma, and I've never met real, live bikers before." A woman with unnaturally red hair was saying this as she pushed forward, practically panting.

"You meet a lot of dead ones?" Orion asked.

"We are so excited to meet you!" Another woman came to stand next to Gladys and her hair was unnaturally blonde. "I'm Henny! I have never seen such delicious specimens of manhood! So, so big and yummy."

Without warning, she spun around and snapped a selfie with us. I saw the picture. She was smiling big as fuck and Orion was scowling like he wanted to kill people and I looked pissed the fuck off.

"Oh, this is perfect. You've got the tough biker look down and you did it without even being told!"

"We should all get a picture!" a fourth lady exclaimed. Her hair was somewhere between gray and purple and her lips were bright orange. "Are either one or both of you into cougars, by any chance? Asking for a friend."

Then the women -- except for one -- crowded around us and asked the one woman who stood back to take pictures.

"I'm not sure --" Elowyn tried to say, but with a shrug, the woman standing back lifted her phone and took pictures, and I could only hope Orion wouldn't pull his gun.

"Don't smile boys!" one of them pressed against us said. "We want you to try and look tough."

Not smiling was no problem.

"Oh, we totally need a biker book this week. Raunchy biker sex is the best! They get me all hot and bothered and poor Stan just can't keep up when I get like that."

"Yes!" another one called out. "Bikers are always hung like horses and down to fuck. I got that expression from my granddaughter."

"Oh, my God!" yet another shouted. "Next week, we should all come to book club dressed as club whores!"

That started a chorus of agreement.

"OK, I think that's enough pictures," Elowyn broke in. "Ladies, your five-minute debate topic today is who makes better book lovers: bikers, athletes, Doms or mafia men? In fact, let's make it ten minutes today."

"So nice to meet you boys," they all called some variation of that to Orion and me as Elowyn shooed them back to their seats.

Orion looked confused as hell, and I felt like I'd just been attacked by the perfume bitches trying to spray shit on you in the mall. While the women debated their topic, Elowyn herded us to the other side of the store.

"Why are you here?" she asked us quietly.

"We came here as customers," I said. "But I kind of feel like a piece of meat now."

That made my girl smile. "They're my book club ladies. They're interesting."

"Ladies my ass," Orion grunted. "I thought the one was about to grab my dick.

"They're all talk," Wyn said. "I'm pretty sure they wouldn't touch you."

I wasn't so sure about that, so I switched topics.

"Elowyn," I said, " We came in because we needed some books on suddenly discovering you're a father. Of a seven-year-old."

Wyn paled and stepped away from me fast, her eyes filling with tears. I stepped right after her, realizing how that sounded.

"Oh, fuck, Elowyn, not me. It's not for me. It's for Orion."

Her hand went to her stomach and she looked slightly less sick. "Really?"

"Really, Wyn. Orion found out a couple months ago after you left that he's got a seven-year-old boy."

She swallowed, the color slowly seeping back into her cheeks. "How's Kadie doing with that news?"

I could feel the anger rolling off Orion. "She disappeared," he said flatly.

I gave her a slight head shake before she could follow up. "Do you have any self-help books like that in stock, Elowyn? Or could you order some for him?"

"We have some parenting books in this section," she said, shifting into book seller mode, and we followed her three rows of shelves toward the back of the store. "As you can see, not a huge selection, but this is a general parenting book, with a section on specific challenges for each age up to twelve. Tells you how to talk to them at each age, how to ask them questions and what you can expect them to do, roughly, at each age."

Orion took the book she offered from her hands.

"What does he like to do?" she asked Orion. "Does he have any particular traits -- do you need a book on raising a creative child? Is he super smart? Because that could be raising a gifted child. Is he athletic? There are all sorts of books for the different aptitudes your child shows."

"Got no idea what he likes. He's a kid. That's about all I know."

Elowyn looked a little surprised at that. "Oh, OK, then here's a book about becoming the parent that you'd like to be. Maybe this one on developing your child's mind. And maybe this one on raising a happy, mentally strong child."

"That's a shit ton of reading," Orion grumbled.

"It's an important job," Elowyn chided him. "You don't want to mess it up because it's a little child you're dealing with and if you get it wrong now, your child will be paying for it later."

"I'll take all of 'em," he said grudgingly.

"And I'll look up some other titles for you that might help," she promised. "Since you're in town for a while."

"Thanks, Wyn," Orion said.

Wyn cashed him out just as the old ladies got up to hit the Romance section.

"We're going with Riding His Throbbing Bike," one of the ladies called to Wyn.

"Excellent choice," she called back.

"Can I see you soon, Wyn?" I asked her softly.

"Yeah, actually I was going to call you tonight to ask if you could come over Saturday night. I need to talk with you."

"Six OK? Can I bring dinner?"

"Sure," she said.

"I'll look forward to it," I said.

"It's not going to be a fun talk," she said, her face tight. "I have a lot to get off my chest."

I leaned toward her. "I don't care if you spend the whole night screaming at me about all the ways I wronged you. No less than I deserve and if it helps make you feel any better at all, you can do whatever the fuck you want, Elowyn."

Taking a piece of paper from inside my cut, I slid a slip of paper across the counter to her. "Would you mind ordering these books for me? Just let me know when they're in and I'll pick them up. Rather give my business to your store than anywhere else."

She looked at my list and nodded, but she still looked tense.

"Wyn."

She looked up at me.

"I can take it. Whatever you need to say, I hope you say it all. I'll be there Saturday, right at six. You need me before then, just give me a call."

"Brother, they're heading our way, and I don't like the looks in their eyes," Orion said from a few feet behind me when he noticed the ladies coming at us.

"See you, Wyn," I said, and then we beat it out of there before they could surround us again.

CHAPTER 19 (ELOWYN): HOLD ON

* ** TW for graphic discussion of domestic violence and child abuse ***

Roberta had met with me twice in the last week, and each conversation with her had left me feeling raw.

Exposed.

Unburdened.

Lighter, amazingly, as if I'd just shrugged out of a three hundred pound backpack I'd been carrying for my entire life.

Before we'd met the first time, Roberta had said we'd just talk and it wouldn't be anything official or clinical or scary.

"I'm a retired therapist," she'd said. "Happily retired. But I've felt so strongly for a while that you needed someone to talk with, Elowyn. I'm good at listening, and I might have some insights, some suggestions that may help you. But mostly, I'll just listen. Sometimes, simply telling your story helps enormously. It's a good first step forward, away from the past. So we can talk, if you want. I'll talk with you as a friend who also happens to be a therapist. And then you may decide down the line that you want to speak with someone officially."

I wanted to talk with her. I couldn't imagine talking to a stranger.

The first time we'd talked, I'd filled her in on my childhood. It helped that her eyes didn't fill with pity or horror. They'd just remained kind and steady.

The second time, I'd filled her in on my adult years up through Lachlan.

That time, it helped that her eyes didn't fill with disgust or condemnation at my behavior. They just remained calm and compassionate.

"So I wasn't enough for him," I finished and at that, her face changed and she leaned forward.

"I'm going to tell you something straight, and if you don't hear anything else, hear this: his cheating had nothing to do with you. It was something from inside him. Think about it this way -- your refusal to marry him stemmed from your childhood, from the things that happened to you, from the example your mother gave you. I suspect, based on what you've told me about his journey to fix himself, that his cheating came from something from his past. That's not on you, Wyn. It's never on you if someone cheats. It comes from something inside them that's broken."

"That makes a lot of sense. It's just hard to believe."

"Believe it. Have you ever really broken that down for Lachlan?"

"Not really. No."

"You've talked to me twice now. And I hope we can talk some more. But maybe think about talking with Lachlan about this. I'm not saying you should, or you have to; I'm just saying think about it."

"I actually have been thinking about talking to him for a while. Ever since he opened up to me about his past, it made me think that we...well, we talked about everything but our pasts when we were together. And we definitely should have talked about them. It might not have made a difference, but maybe it would have."

Roberta gave me a half smile. "It's always hard to say. But both of you had some issues to overcome that left you two in a constant cycle of hurt."

She wasn't wrong, so when Lach and Orion had walked into the book store unexpectedly, it'd seemed like a sign. Without thinking about it too much, I'd asked Lach to dinner, which was why I was now opening my door to him.

"Brought some comfort food for tonight," he said seriously, holding up two bags from a really good local rib place. The man knew my weaknesses.

We got settled at my little table, and I tried to start eating -- the ribs smelled wonderful -- but I was nervous with all the dark thoughts in my head. Picking at my food, I felt Lach's eyes on me.

"You hurt me."

We both froze at my soft words. Lach because he thought we were having dinner before we started talking, and me because that wasn't what I had practiced saying at all. But I'd started and, we were both about to discover, we were in the midst of an avalanche of emotions we couldn't outrun.

"You hurt me." That came out stronger, and I looked at him instead of my plate this time.

"You hurt me. You hurt me, Lach, for years. You hurt me, and I know I agreed to it, but it hurt. And it hurt more and more the longer it went on, and I wanted you to stop because I wanted you to be the one person in my life who never hurt me."

His eyes watched me, but he didn't say anything, didn't try to interrupt because he knew what was coming, and what was coming was everything I'd never told him.

"My mom...she used to get beat. Beaten by whatever man was in her life. She kept picking losers that hurt her, and they'd hurt me, too. They'd smack her around, and then, when I couldn't stop screaming or crying, they'd hit me. Sometimes they'd knock me into a wall, sometimes they'd hit me so hard I'd need stitches, a couple of times they broke my arms, sometimes they'd kick me so hard I flew across the room and I had big bruises that would hurt for days."

I swallowed back the tears, kind of missing the days when he and I never discussed our childhoods.

"Mom never stopped them. Never. She just told me to never tie myself to a man because they always hurt you, and as long as you weren't married, you could get away clean. And she'd take me to some person in the neighborhood who'd stitch me up, stitch her up, but sometimes I had to go to the hospital or she did. And we'd lie about what happened. Since we moved around, I never had broken bones in the same hospital system twice."

Looking down at my plate, I saw I'd shredded my napkin.

"Some of the men seemed nice at first, and I could see hope in Mom's eyes, but then they weren't so nice and it would start again. I can remember thinking with each new guy she brought home that maybe this guy would actually be nice. I just wanted a dad like other girls had. I wanted somebody to love me because it didn't feel like my mom loved me if she let them hurt me. When I got older, I kind of gave up on that and lowered the bar, thinking maybe if someone would even just care about me, I'd be happy."

I forced my hands to relax, noting I'd clenched them into fists.

"And when I hit high school, I found that guys would be nice to me if I was nice to them, but the minute it was over, it was like it never happened, until the next time they wanted sex. And I was always willing, hoping somebody would care. I was always willing, Lach. I was that girl in school, the easy one, the one who actually slept with every guy on every team. I got called names, but names didn't hurt as much as fists, and for a few minutes, I could pretend that I was with someone who cared for me. I was still doing that when I met you. You saw it. And you didn't care that I was a slut."

"You weren't a slut, Wyn. Don't ever call yourself that." His voice was gentle, but stern. Maybe edging toward angry that I would refer to myself like that.

"You had the kindest eyes of anyone I was ever with. You sat and talked to me at the bar. You got to know me -- except where my past was concerned -- and I fell in love with you. I needed you to be the one person who didn't hurt me, but you did, Lachlan. Over and over and over again."

My voice was getting loud but Lach was still watching me, his eyes agonized. Unable to sit still, I jumped up and Lachlan did, too, staying right with me, right in front of me, giving me a target.

"You hurt me and you wouldn't let me talk to you about it! I wanted to be the only woman in your life. I wanted to be the only one!"

I made an incoherent noise and stepped closer to him, forcing myself to look into his eyes, which had tears in them.

"You hurt me, Lachlan. You hurt me and you wouldn't let me talk about it!" I'd never yelled at Lach like that in my life. "You wouldn't let me talk about it!"

"Because I didn't want to have to make a choice!" he yelled, but he wasn't yelling at me. I knew that. It was something pushed down deep in him that erupted from him loudly. It was his pain and fear finally coming into the light.

It was the same way he'd reacted when I wouldn't answer his texts after I sent the picture of Yomi in his arms. His texts that came in before I left were angry, demanding, something that was unlike Lach. I'd scared him when I sent that picture, when, in effect, I'd slapped him in the face with not believing he cared for me. He'd been panicking.

He took a deep breath. "Because I couldn't lose you, Wyn. And I knew if you said stop, I'd have to stop or lose you and I didn't know if I could stop. I didn't understand the need for control then. I want to think I would have stopped, I even told you that I would have, I want to think we could have worked it out if given the chance, but I didn't know for sure, so I couldn't risk you asking."

"So you just kept hurting me!"

"I did, Wyn."

"You hurt me."

"I did, Wyn." He cradled my cheeks in his hands. "I did, Wyn, and I'm so damn sorry." His remorse underscored every broken syllable as tears dripped down his cheeks.

"You hurt me. You hurt me! Youhurtmeyouhurtmeyouhurtme!" I was screaming by now, and Lachlan just grabbed me close while I screamed and cried against his chest. I was screaming at my mother; I was screaming at her many boyfriends; I was screaming at the hundreds and hundreds of guys I'd had sex with; I was screaming at Lachlan.

After a while, I stopped screaming, but I couldn't stop crying, and Lach held me and eventually sunk to the floor, cradling me on his lap. He held me tight, not saying a word, just holding me against his heart while I let it all out, his hand rubbing my back. It could have been hours; it could have been days. But eventually, the tears slowed and I calmed, my breathing eventually returning to normal with the occasional shuddering breath.

"Your legs," I finally managed to speak. "They have to be numb by now."

"I don't give a fuck about my legs, Elowyn. I'll hold you forever," his gravelly voice promised in my ear. "Please, let me have this. Let me just hold you."

How ironic that the man who'd broken my heart was now the one holding it together.

Holding me together.

Holding me.

Holding on.

And sometimes, healing can begin just by knowing that someone, despite everything, is willing to hold on.

We were like tiny seedlings pushing their way up through the dirt in the spring.

Delicate.

Fragile.

Struggling.

But doing our best to hold on.

CHAPTER 20 (Lachlan): IT'S ALL DARKNESS

Elowyn fell asleep in my lap, and I just continued to hold her for a while, not knowing if I'd ever have the chance again given what she'd told me tonight. Given the many and various heartaches she'd unleashed. Given the way I'd added to her hurt by hurting her so badly.

She'd fallen asleep in the arms of a man who was just one of many assholes who'd hurt her. Never had I hurt her physically, but who's to say which is worse? I'd been in fights, been punched, been kicked and it hurt, but the bodily part of it healed. Then I thought of the shit I carried inside. That hurt, too, but it hadn't healed.

I was working on it, facing it, but that shit left scars. Wyn carried scars, too, and I thought of many of my brothers. Maybe all of us, in one way or another, carried scars inside, and maybe that was better because we could hide them from others. We could act normal and not let others see all the ways we'd been carved up with pain.

But after holding her for so long, when she squirmed slightly in my arms, trying to find a more comfortable position, I decided she really needed her bed. So I stood up with Wyn, not letting go of her until I absolutely had to, and carried her to her bed. I flipped the soft comforter and sheet aside and laid her down in the bed, making sure to pull her socks off. She never once slept in socks when we'd been together, no matter how cold it got, and I was betting that hadn't changed. I pulled the comforter up to her chin and her eyes fluttered open.

"Don't go," she said, her voice raspy from all the tears and the screaming. "Just stay with me tonight. Please."

For a moment, I looked at her and then nodded, and her eyes drifted close with the assurance that I'd stay and she wouldn't be alone.

"Thank you, Lachlan," she whispered.

Anything for you, Wyn. But I was afraid, especially after what I'd discovered tonight, that I'd learned the lesson too late.

If Wyn couldn't sleep with socks on, I couldn't sleep with a shirt on. Pulling off my socks, cut and shirt, I walked around to the other side of the bed and got under the covers. At some point in the night, I came awake. I was on my side, my hand splayed over Wyn's stomach, and she was on her back, pressed right against me, sound asleep. I bent my arm up and rested my head in my hand, staring down at Elowyn.

You hurt me.

I wasn't a man who cried in front of others, ever, but sometimes at night when I was alone in bed, I let the tears come. Every night after I fucked around on Wyn, I'd stayed at the club house because of guilt and because I cried.

Looked like tonight was going to be one of those nights, and that scared the hell out of me because it'd be easy to lose it tonight, easily the hardest night of my life; I couldn't speak for Wyn, but maybe it had been for her, too. I could feel the tears forming even as I thought about Wyn's soft voice uttering those three words at the beginning of our conversation.

You hurt me.

I would rather have been a guest in the MC's guest room and have Butcher use every single fucking tool we had at our disposal on me than have to come face to face with how much and how deeply I'd hurt Wyn. No torture could come close to the pain I felt holding my screaming, crying Elowyn in my arms as she let it out.

My Elowyn.

No matter if she was done with me forever, I'd never stop loving her. But I was my fucking father all over again. He'd hurt me, and I'd hurt Wyn, the woman I loved, and not even his fists had ever hurt me like her pain tonight had torn into me. I hadn't sat down on the floor to hold her as much as I could no longer stay upright with the weight of her pain forcing my knees to give out.

You hurt me. You hurt me, Lach, for years. You hurt me, and I know I agreed to it, but it hurt. And it hurt more and more the longer it went on, and I wanted you to stop because I wanted you to be the one person in my life who never hurt me.

The tears were pouring out of my eyes now, dripping onto Wyn's neck, her chest, her arm.

You hurt me. Youhurtmeyouhurtmeyouhurtme.

Once tears start, it's hard as hell to stop them and maybe we shouldn't. Maybe it's OK to let them come, maybe each tear is mining some of the pain inside of us and carrying it away, outside of us. Each of my tears fell silently onto Wyn, and it wasn't a baptism so much as it was a cleansing. I was hoping the tears could somehow wash away some of the hurt I'd brought into her life.

I cried for a long damn time for the ways I'd hurt this woman, silently, though, so I wouldn't wake her, but inside I was yelling and screaming the way she'd done, only I was crying out I'm sorry, Wyn. I'm so damn sorry.

Once the tears stopped, I fell asleep with my Wyn tucked against me. In the morning, I woke up the second she stirred and she gave me a solemn good morning.

"I always slept better with you," she said.

"Same," I told her, and I meant it.

"Thank you for staying," she said.

"Thank you for asking. It was the best night I've had since you left."

She declined breakfast with me, saying she needed some time to think before she headed into work, and I kissed her head and tapped the tip of her nose when we stood at her door.

"I'm going back home for two days," I said. "I'll try not to bother you. Give you some time. But call me if you need me, OK?"

She nodded.

"I love you, Wyn," I said. "I just need you to understand that. I think you're the strongest woman I know, and I'm sorry you had to be stronger because of me. And even though I can't be the man who never hurt you, I'd like to be the man who learned his lesson and who loved you like you've never been loved before in the way you always deserved."

A day later, I was back at the club house.

Six men stared at me from our guest room.

Butcher stood next to me.

"Gentlemen, thank you for joining us today. Let's get right to it: you're all gathered here because I find each of you to be abusive assholes and we're going to fight, not because that will make up for what you've done, but because that will make me happy as fuck to see you six get back a little bit of what you dealt out."

"Oh, yeah. Real fair. Two of you and six of us and you both look like you're giants on steroids," one of them said.

"No," I said. "He's just a bystander and won't be interfering. Six of you, all at once, against me."

"I'm just here to rip your hearts out of your chests and eat them once he beats you to death," Butcher said. Then he smiled at them and the fuckers just about pissed themselves.

"I think you all remember Elowyn," I said, my voice suddenly serious. "Pretty little girl, sweet, her mother's only child."

At my girl's name, they all froze, suddenly understanding that this was not just retribution but Retribution.

I opened the file folder I held in my hands and detailed each man's crimes against Wyn. When I finished, I looked up at them.

"So now you know why you're here. We need to get started because I have things to do and Butcher skipped breakfast today so he's hungry as hell."

They didn't move.

"OK, guys, that was your cue to attack."

"Don't do this, man," one of them said, shaking. "I'm begging you --"

"I imagine Wyn cried and asked you to stop a couple of times, but you didn't, so...you can either stand there and let me do to you what you did to her, or you can give taking me down your best shot. Up to you."

"Fuck this," another man said and he rushed me, the others following suit, thinking to overwhelm me with their numbers.

And then it began. Even six to one, it was an unfair fight. Mayhem brothers were trained by the best...or maybe the worst, depending on your viewpoint...and I took the six of them on and even toyed with them a while until I got bored and ended each asshole, one after the other. All of them died with broken noses, broken arms, broken ribs.

It didn't change anything. Their deaths didn't erase what had happened to Wyn, but they couldn't hurt anyone else now -- and they had all left a long string of hurt in their wake, right up to the present day.

I stood looking down at the bodies for a minute.

Butcher looked at me.

"Better?"

"Not really," I said. "Got a ways to go, I think."

"Get your light back, Shadow. Otherwise, it's all darkness."

Then he walked out, and I was wondering if I'd just hallucinated that shit.